Egmont Passage:

Tale Of The Seventh Mystery

Antonino Fabiano

Original cover art and illustrations by Tim Kelley. Production layout and graphic design by Mark Robichaux. Author's photograph by Larry Fabiano.

Printed in Victoria, Canada

A cataloguing record for this book that includes the U.S. Library of Congress Classification number, the Library of Congress Call number and the Dewey Decimal cataloguing code is available from the National Library of Canada. The complete cataloguing record can be obtained from the National Library's online database at: www.nlc-bnc.ca/amicus/index-e.html

ISBN: 1-4120-1324-0

Published by Tidal Tales Publishing in cooperation with:

TRAFFORD

This book was published **on-demand** in cooperation with Trafford Publishing. On-demand publishing is a unique process and service of making a book available for retail sale to the public taking advantage of on-demand manufacturing and Internet marketing. **On-demand publishing** includes promotions, retail sales, manufacturing, order fulfilment, accounting and collecting royalties on behalf of the author.

Suite 6E, 2333 Government St., Victoria, B.C. V8T 4P4, CANADA

Phone	250-383-6864	Toll-free	1-888-232-4444 (Canada & US)
Fax	250-383-6804	E-mail	sales@trafford.com
Web site	www.trafford.com	TRAFFORD PUBLISHING IS A DIVISION OF TRAFFORD HOLDINGS LTD.	
Trafford Catalogue #03-1702		www.trafford.com/robots/03-1702.html	

10   9   8   7   6   5   4   3

For J.J. Frost...
May Your Unfinished Adventure Continue Through These Pages...

*"**Life** is a journey. Make fun of it."*

Author Unknown

Acknowledgments

Thanks to all those who helped make this book a reality: To the administration, teachers, staff, and students at Johnson Middle School in Bradenton. Special thanks to Treva Anderson, Ellen Binder, Pat Kantor, and Carol Timmons for reading the manuscript and providing constructive comments. To students Vanessa Guererro, Jordon VonBorstel, and my entire 2002-2003 Accelerated Reader class for encouragement and excellent suggestions. Also thanks to Roy Larson, Susan Johnson, and Van Edwards for your support throughout the school year. To General Colin L. Powell (USA, Ret) for inspired leadership during my Pentagon days; thanks for lending your "rules to live by." To Jim Schulte and Accounting Company. To Mark Caldwell and the staff at *Tierra Verde Property Management*; thanks Mark for your friendship and "lending me your ear" during the writing process. To Francis Bernard and Richard Haerther for your proofreading expertise. To Tim Kelley and *TNT Designs* for great suggestions, creative energy, and exceptional original artwork. To *Tropical Views* for excellent support and valuable column space. To Sally Yoder for sharing sage advice, a winning spirit, and "can-do" attitude. To Mark Robichaux for excellent production and layout design, enthusiasm, and your friendship. To my parents, sister Tina, and brother Steve for love and support. To my brother Larry and *Gabriel's Moving Service* of Tallahassee for sound business advice. Finally to my children Joey, Keri Lee, and Tara Nicole; you rock my world!

Nino

TABLE OF CONTENTS

ONE
MR. CELI'S FIELD TRIP (2004)
1

TWO
LETTER OF MARQUE
3

THREE
FORT DESOTO
7

FOUR
THE GOLD DOUBLOON
9

FIVE
WELL, NOW WHAT?
11

SIX
GOING NATIVE (Prehistoric Florida)
14

SEVEN
TAILS THE TRAILS
19

EIGHT
THE SPANISH FLEET (1528)
23

NINE
PANFILO DE NARVAEZ
27

TEN
BUNCE'S PASS
31

ELEVEN
MAKING CAMP
33

TWELVE
TRUE CONFESSIONS
36

THIRTEEN
THE GREAT GALE (1848)
43

FOURTEEN
THE SHERROD EDWARDS
46

FIFTEEN
PLAYING TURTLE
49

SIXTEEN
BILLY BAREFOOT (1861)
52

SEVENTEEN
LITTLE VICTORIA
55

EIGHTEEN
THE MYSTERY CLUES
57

NINETEEN
LIFE IS A JOURNEY
64

TWENTY
THE EGMONT PASSAGE
66

TWENTY ONE
TEMPEST IN A TEACUP
70

TWENTY TWO
FLAT WATER
72

TWENTY THREE
PIRATES!
74

TWENTY FOUR
GHOST RIDER
76

TWENTY FIVE
COLD HARBOR
78

TWENTY SIX
THE FRENCH PIRATE REDUX
80

TWENTY SEVEN
HARDTACK
82

TWENTY EIGHT
JUAN JON LOPEZ
86

TWENTY NINE
THE VOODOO PIRATE'S CURSE
91

THIRTY
PIRATE LOOKS AT 14
93

THIRTY ONE
"RIGHT ON SCHEDULE"
96

THIRTY TWO
PIRATE PRISONERS **(1898)**
99

THIRTY THREE
THE "ROUGH RIDERS"
102

THIRTY FOUR
I CAN SEE KLEARLY
104

THIRTY FIVE
"IT'S IN THE EYES"
109

THIRTY SIX
"SOMEONE SPECIAL"
113

THIRTY SEVEN
KERMIT THE HERMIT
115

THIRTY EIGHT
OLD FORT DADE (1996)
121

THIRTY NINE
THE SEVENTH MYSTERY
124

FORTY
TALE OF THE MYSTERY DOUBLOON (2004)
128

EPILOGUE
132

TIMELINE
134

NOTE TO MY READERS
138

ABOUT THE AUTHOR
140

Chapter One

Mr. Celi's Field Trip
(2004)

The *Foul Belle* bounced on the wake of two passing jet skis. Mr. Celi's students, riding the converted shrimp boat, rocked side-to-side. Disturbed by the rocking motion, JJ looked up from his book. *The Gulf was unusually busy for a Friday,* he thought. A merchant ship, led by a pilot boat, carefully navigated his large vessel between the broad pillars of the Sunshine Skyway Bridge.

On the horizon sail boats caught the morning breeze and skimmed across the waves. One particular ship, about 100 yards off shore, caught JJ's attention. Unlike the other sailboats that had taken advantage of the northerly winds, the old Spanish galleon had its sails and anchors down. The Egmont Lighthouse, seven miles in the distance, blinked steadily through the empty masts of the galleon.

JJ reached for the binoculars in his knapsack. "GhostRider," he whispered, reading the name on the ship. A crew member raised the *Jolie Rouge* flag, while another sailor, peering through a spyglass, waved back at JJ. Gasparilla Days were fast approaching, JJ remembered. *Probably some businessmen playing buccaneers for the day,* he thought, with a pang of jealousy.

The *Foul Belle*, still smelling of shrimp, vibrated to an abrupt halt at the gulf pier. Mr. Celi led his social studies students off the weathered dock toward *Pavillion 29* at the Fort DeSoto County Park.

With the Gulf of Mexico to the West, and Boca Ciega and Tampa Bay to the South and East, Fort DeSoto was an ideal location for its former mission. *Built in 1898, and now surrounded by mangroves, palm trees and a huge bike path, the fort once defended the mainland from an invading Spanish Armada. When the attack never came, Fort DeSoto was abandoned and turned into a tourist attraction.*

"Come on, JJ," Isabella pleaded. "We're already late. Mr. Celi's going to give us another detention. Come on."

"Okay, okay, I'm coming." JJ broke from his daydream. He closed the book on his lap, *A Florida Field Guide To Naval History,* and picked up the knapsack sitting on the wooden bench. "It'll just be another one of Mr. Celi's boring field trips."

"Boring or not, Mr. Celi's going to give us another detention," Zeke threatened. He scribbled a note on his tablet.

"What are you doing, Zeke?" JJ folded his reading glasses and placed them in his cargo shorts. He ran down the gangplank toward the sandy path where Isabella and Zeke waited.

"I promised Mr. Celi I'd write a story about the field trip for the school paper." Zeke shook his head. "But how can I write anything if I miss half of what he has to say?"

"Mr. Celi will just fill our heads with useless history dates and facts. Then he'll give us a test. You can quote me on it. Put *that* in the *Tidal Tales Telegraph.*" JJ adjusted his Tampa Bay Buccaneer hat. "I want the real stuff. Give me pirates, corsairs...Give me adventure..."

"Just be careful what you wish for...because you just may get it." Isabella laughed, her blonde hair waving in the cool breeze.

"...Even as a kid," JJ smiled, "I imagined I was Gasparilla, or some other pirate, exploring the Gulf of Mexico. Or maybe the Caribbean. I would have been a *good* pirate, though. Not like Black Bart or Blackbeard. I'd only be stealing from the rich. Would give the money to the poor. You know, like Robin Hood of the High Seas. I guess I was born a couple hundred years too late..."

"You're such a dreamer. That's what I love about you, JJ Lopez." Isabella smiled. "But sometimes I think you live way too much in the past..."

"Come on, *Robin Hood of the High Seas,* we gotta hurry." Zeke pushed the notepad in his back pocket. "Mr. Celi will have another one of his fits if we're late."

Chapter Two

The Letter Of Marque

The class assembled at *Pavillion 29*. A group of adults, some dressed in colorful pirate costumes, picnicked in a nearby pavilion. JJ, Isabella, and Zeke arriving late to *Pavillion 29*, were greeted by Mr. Celi's admonishing glare.

"Got lost in my reading," JJ apologized, raising the *Field Guide* in the air. "Sorry. Just lost track of time."

"Glad you three Bayway Buccaneers could grace us with your presence," Mr. Celi answered sarcastically. He turned to the other students. "Come on kids. Gather closely. I don't want to have to shout."

The students bunched together like sardines in a tin.

"You stink," insulted Sally Jane. She moved away from Charlie. "Get away from me."

"Yeah," sniffed another girl. "You smell like a bucket of dead shrimp."

"You smell worse than I do." Charlie shoved her. "Only its not the bad smell from the *Foul Belle*. You smell like a girl." The boys laughed, slapping each other on the back.

"They're so childish," Isabella said in disgust. She pulled back her curly blonde hair. "I'm glad you and Zeke aren't that way."

"Okay, Buccaneers. That's enough of that." Mr. Celi grabbed the whistle dangling from his neck. He gave it a hard blow. "Let me have your attention please. I want you to have fun today. But I expect you all to be on your best behavior. You know how hard it is for me to get a field trip approved for the *Bayway Island Boarding School,* especially after what happened during our visit to the Salvadore Dali Museum last year..."

"Yeah," Charlie shouted. "JJ and Zeke got locked in one of the back rooms of the museum. The cops searched everywhere trying to find them..."

"It really wasn't our fault," JJ insisted.

The students broke into laughter.

"And then Mr. Celi had to call an ambulance because Zeke fainted from all the excitement..." Sally Jane gave Zeke an accusing smile.

"Oh, gawd," Zeke sneered. "Do you always have to mention that?"

"Okay. Okay. That's enough, students." Mr. Celi interrupted. "Remember, this is still a school day so you Buccaneers still have an assignment to complete..."

The students gave a loud groan.

"That's not fair," one student protested. "Field trips are supposed to be fun."

"Yeah," the crowd echoed. "It's not fair."

"Okay, kids. That's enough complaining. Please settle down." Mr. Celi lifted his hand in the air, like a traffic cop. Stepping onto an old tree trunk, he continued his short speech. "This is a fun assignment. Actually it's a local history trivia game I found on a web site. I think you'll enjoy it..."

"See I told you, Izzy," JJ whispered. "Like I said stupid history facts."

"Shhh." Isabella placed a finger over her lips. "Don't be rude."

"Do we have to do it?" complained one student.

"You've already been separated into teams." Mr. Celi ignored the complaints. "Each team will be given a copy of this *Letter of Marque...*" He waved a handful of letters in the air.

"I thought this was going to be a fun day," protested Charlie.

"What's a *Letter of Marque,*" Zeke asked.

The students broke into a roar of laughter.

"Ezekiel," Mr. Celi took a long pause. He turned to JJ and Isabella, then back to Zeke. "If you and the other Bayway Buccaneers were more punctual to class you would not miss out on so much of your studies." Turning away, he asked, "Would someone like to tell Ezekiel the importance of the letter?"

Sally Jane raised her hand and recited from memory. "*Letters of Marque* were issued by kings and queens. A *Letter of Marque* gave pirates the license to legally steal from merchant ships. The letters also allowed pirates to keep half of everything they stole. These pirates were called privateers because..."

"Very good, Sally," Mr. Celi interrupted. "Your *Letter of Marque*, the one I've given you, is kind of like a *hall pass*. It allows you to roam Old Fort DeSoto in search of the answers to the mystery clues. Of course, you won't be doing any plundering like the pirates did." Mr. Celi laughed at his own humor.

The students erupted into mock laughter.

"As I said, each letter has a mystery clue. Six of them, actually." Mr. Celi handed the letters out. "On the back of the *Letter of Marque* is a map of the old fort and the local islands. You may use the map to help answer the mystery clues..."

"Can we ask you for the answers?" JJ grinned sarcastically. "Will you give them to us and save us some time?"

"With the exception of me..." Mr. Celi glared at JJ. "you may use any resource you like. You may even use your book." He paused, then changed the subject. "The first team to give me the six correct answers will win the grand prize..."

"What's that?" Sally Jane called out eagerly. "What's the prize?"

"Well, the annual Gasparilla Days celebration is coming up in a week," Mr. Celi glanced at the pirates in the next pavilion. "You can already see they're getting into costume for the big event. Soon everyone in the bay area will be celebrating Jose Gaspar's invasion of Tampa Bay." Mr. Celi turned back to his students. "The first team that gets all six correct mystery answers will be honorary guests of the mayor. You'll sit in the grandstand to watch the 2004 Gasparilla parade. And you'll get out of school for the afternoon to meet Gasparilla and the other pirates..."

The students exploded in cheers and laughter.

A pirate from the nearby pavilion walked toward the group of students. "Excuse moi, captain teacher."

Mr. Celi turned to the beaded pirate. "Yes. May I help you?"

"Oui. With your permission..." The pirate spoke with a French accent. He raised his arm draped with rainbow colored beads. "...My friends over there, and I....we're planning an adventure... Since you're already here...we thought your crewe might like a few beads..."

"Please go right ahead. I'm sure my kids will enjoy them." Mr. Celi turned back to his students. "One more thing. It's 9 a.m. You have three hours to solve the mystery clues.."

The pirate meandered through the crowd of students. "Here's a turquoise one for you, my pretty lady."

5

Isabella blushed. "Thank you sir."

"And for you young man," he turned to JJ. "how about a nice purple one? I feel sure I'll be seeing you very soon..."

"You mean the Gasparilla Parade?" JJ placed the beads around his neck. "Sure do hope so. I'd love to go!"

"Excuse me, sir," Zeke pulled out his notebook and pen. "I'm Zeke. I'm writing an article on our field trip for the *Tidal Tales Telegraph*...mind if I mention you in the story?"

"Not at all, Zeke....here are some beads to match your cap." He handed Zeke an orange and blue beaded necklace. The pirate then tightened the belt around his faded blue overcoat. "I am the famous French pirate of the open seas...When you're finished here come join me and my friends...we'll have a chat!"

The pirate gave a set of beads to Sally Jane and Charlie before returning to his pirate friends.

Zeke leaned into JJ, then whispered. "Pretty convincing pirate, huh?"

"Yeah." JJ fingered the purple beads. "I think he believed it himself."

"Okay, guys. If I can have your attention one more time. When you hear this." Mr. Celi blew the whistle. "Everyone will meet here at *pavilion 29*. After lunch I'll announce the winner of the game."

"We won't have to go back to school after lunch, will we?" Sally Jane said hopefully.

"Actually, no. I have a special surprise for everyone. I was going to wait until later to tell you. But since you asked..." Mr. Celi smiled, pointing to the tiny island on the Gulf of Mexico. "After lunch we'll take the *Foul Belle* out to Egmont Key for a tour of old Fort Dade and the lighthouse. I've also arranged for you to meet some of the harbor pilots. You know, the ship captains that guide the huge ships under the Sunshine Skyway Bridge..."

The students cheered and shouted.

"Now if there are no other questions..." Mr. Celi blew the whistle. "You may begin."

The students scrambled off, forming into their teams. Mr. Celi called to JJ, Isabella, and Zeke. "Remember, meet me here at noon. I expect you Bayway Buccaneers to be prompt!"

Chapter Three

Fort DeSoto

JJ darted up toward the old artillery battery on the old fort. "Wait up," Isabella said breathlessly, trying hard to catch up.

"Can you imagine what it must have been like during pirate times?" JJ walked the grassy berm on Battery Laidley. He pointed toward the gleaming waters of the Gulf of Mexico. A cool February breeze rustled through the palms. "Sailing ships. Endless sea adventures. Guess I'm an over-14 victim of fate..."

"...Don't be so dramatic. You've been listening to too much of that Parrothead music." Isabella shook her head. "Pirate life is not for me. I like the comforts of the 21 century."

"Actually, I don't want to imagine it, either." Zeke shouted breathlessly, running hard to catch up to JJ and Isabella.

"Hey," JJ reached a hand, pulling Zeke up the grass hill. "how'd the interview go?"

"Learn any interesting stuff from the French pirate?" Isabella laughed.

"I learned that I would never want to live

7

during the days of pirates. Those guys are crazy!" Zeke answered, taking a deep breath. "And to get to your question, JJ, I'd be scared to live during the pirate era. I'm African American, remember? My ancestors were slaves on some of those pirate ships..."

"You got it all wrong, Zeke," JJ corrected. "it was mostly the governments that supported slavery. But the pirates, they formed a true democracy. They freed the slaves, and gave them a chance to sail with their crews. A guy named Henry Caesar, they called him Black Caesar, he had his own ship and crew..."

"Don't try to make them out as heroes..." Zeke admonished.

"I'm not. Oh, I know many of them were bad. It's just that...," JJ drifted off again. "They must have had great adventures. I must have been a pirate in a previous life. Feels like I sailed these waters all my life. I'll bet I have buried treasure over there," JJ pointed toward Egmont Key. "beneath the shade of the lighthouse."

"Earth to JJ," Zeke rolled his notepad to form a megaphone. "Time to get back to reality."

"Yeah, JJ. Let's work on the mystery clues," Isabella said. She waved the *Letter of Marque* in JJ's face. "Remember our assignment?"

"Let's just forget about school today," JJ protested. "Let's have some fun."

Isabella ignored him, taking a seat on the grassy berm. "Look at the letter. If we put our minds together we can easily solve these clues."

"Maybe we'll sit with the mayor," Zeke said hopefully. "...at the Gasparilla parade next week."

"That would be fun." JJ waved them off. "But you guys go ahead. I have some exploring to do..."

Isabella opened her book bag, taking out a red apple. She unfolded the *Letter of Marque*. "Come on JJ, let's try to solve these clues."

Zeke took out his pen and notepad and playfully wrote a headline, then read it to Isabella. "*Bayway Buccaneers Win Contest, Much To Mr. Celi's Chagrin!* Do you think the St. Petersburg Times will publish that?"

Zeke and Isabella laughed.

Chapter Four

The Gold Doubloon

"Bling, bling." JJ shouted, his voice filled with excitement. He slid the wooden top from the old artesian well, then stood at it's edge. "Hey Izzy, Zeke, take a look at this. Something shiny down there."

"Good grief," Isabella said in clear frustration. "How are we ever going to complete this assignment if you are always running off?" She stuffed the letter into her book bag and hurried toward JJ.

"It's some sort of a coin," JJ leaned into the well. "Maybe it's a Spanish doubloon!"

"There you go, dreaming again. Be careful," Zeke said cautiously. "The ground doesn't look very solid."

"Yeah. It's quite a ways down." Isabella agreed. "Would hate for you to fall in."

"You guys worry too much. This well's been around for years. It's not going anywhere!" JJ sat on the rim of the opening. He strained for a better look. Rocks rolled along the edge, fell into the hole, then splashed in the shallow water below. "What do you think it is?"

"Just a bottle cap." Isabella adjusted the book bag on her shoulders.

"Nah. It's a coin. I'm sure of it." JJ disagreed. He pulled out his pen light. "Not bright enough."

"Come on," Isabella grew impatient. "Let's go."

"Maybe this'll help." JJ pulled out his binoculars.

"Let's get on with this assignment," Isabella pleaded.

9

"Yeah." Zeke turned toward Isabella. "We're probably way behind the others by now."

"You guys go on. I'll catch up to you." JJ stared into the well, focusing his binoculars. "It's gotta be something else, like......"

"Aahhhhhhhhhhhhhhhh.....!" JJ's voice trailed on his last words.

"Oh, gawd!" Zeke shouted, as he fainted, and fell to the ground.

Limestone and sand, once a solid part of the well wall, crumbled beneath JJ's body. He let out a horrific scream as he tumbled into the open pit. His screams were followed by a huge splash. Light swirled in frenzied circles, followed by the deafening sound of total silence.

Chapter Five

Well, Now What?

"**Wake** up, JJ!" Isabella pleaded.

"Are you okay?" Zeke shouted.

"Ouch," JJ screamed, touching his swollen forehead. Still dazed, he sat up in the shallow puddle. "What a headache..."

"That was some fall," Zeke said.

"You all right?" Isabella asked again. She wiped the mud from JJ's face.

"Yeah, I think so. Just a little bruise on the head," JJ answered with more doubt than certainty. He wrung the mud from his shirt sleeve. "How'd you get down here?"

"It wasn't easy." Zeke frowned.

"Yeah. Zeke fainted again." Isabella shook her head. "After he woke up we used the iron hand-steps on the side of the well to get down..."

"Zeke fainted again?" JJ asked, giving Zeke an incredulous look.

"Yeah, sorry." Zeke gave an impish smile.

"I nearly twisted my ankle getting down." Isabella reprimanded. "And you, JJ, you could have really hurt yourself. Now let's get out of here..."

"Look," JJ opened his hand. Wet silt drained between his fingers. "Bling, bling."

"It *is* some sort of coin," Isabella shouted.

"It's a doubloon," JJ corrected.

"Let me have a look. Hey, that's tight!" Zeke screamed with equal enthusiasm, his black face covered in limestone mud. "What's it say?"

"It says, 'Yo Creo, 1528.'" JJ passed the coin to Zeke. "Told you it was a coin."

"The other side has some sort of ship on it." Zeke examined the coin, then handed it to Isabella.

"What do you think it means?" Isabella asked.

"It's Spanish. I'm sure of it." JJ took the coin from Isabella. He used her scrunchy to wipe his reading glasses. Adjusting the glasses on his nose, he added, "Lots of Spanish ships went down in the Gulf of Mexico. Lots of pirates buried treasure on the Bayway Islands, too. But I have no clue as to what *Yo Creo* means." The coin flashed in the rays of the rising sun.

Zeke looked up to the bright opening above. The wet limestone walls glistened. "Think it was dropped in here by accident?"

"I don't know." JJ removed his penlight from his mud-soaked knapsack. "Maybe it washed in during a rainstorm." He took a long pause, flashing the sides of the well with his penlight.

"What else do you have in that backpack?" Isabella laughed curiously.

"Just a change of clothes." JJ answered. "And some beef jerky. Snacks. My book. Binoculars..."

"Okay. We get the picture," Zeke laughed. "You've got everything but the kitchen sink."

"You just never know..." JJ looked up through the well opening. His face turned serious. "We're going to have a heck of a time getting out of here. Those iron hand-steps are quite steep. It's going to be a lot more difficult climbing up...."

"Hey shine your light over there." Isabella pointed toward a hint of light in the distance. "Maybe the water runs out that way? Let's work our way in that direction. It'll be easier."

The Bayway Buccaneers followed the small beam of light aimed on the shallow creek bed. They followed the water toward the distant hollow opening of the aquifer.

"Good thing it's the dry season," Zeke laughed.

"Yeah." JJ swept his tiny penlight across the shallow creek, then up and down the narrow cave walls. "Otherwise we'd be swimming in a cave."

The creek led to a number of aquifer chambers of various sizes. The closer to the cave entrance, the more illuminated the cave became.

"Wow, look at this!" Isabella waded in knee deep water. "Look at these drawings."

JJ shut off his flashlight and splashed his way toward Isabella. The limestone walls were painted with pictures of wild animals. Some had horns. Some tusks. One painting showed a herd of mastodons.

"It's a saber-toothed tiger." JJ pointed to a drawing on the ceiling showing a hunter chasing a cat-like animal.

"Awesome." Zeke ran his fingers along the herd of mastodons painted on the opposite wall. "This is just awesome."

"They look real, don't they?" JJ answered. "This one looks like an ancient deer."

"They do," Isabella said. "Probably some kids having a little fun..."

"No. I mean they are real," JJ protested. "I think they're authentic."

"There you go again," Isabella smiled. "You have such a great imagination."

"Izzy's right," Zeke laughed. "They can't be real. If they were," he took a long pause, "well, they'd be worth millions."

"Besides," Isabella added. "Someone would have already discovered them by now."

"They're from the prehistoric era," JJ insisted. "I have this feeling. I really do. You guys never believe me..."

"This is nonsense, JJ." Isabella headed for the cave opening. "Let's get out of here. Mr. Celi and the others are probably worried sick about us."

"I agree," Zeke smiled. "I'll race you to the opening!"

Zeke and Isabella charged the cave opening, their arms flapping in reckless abandon. What they saw next left them breathless.

Chapter Six

Going Native
(Prehistoric Florida)

For *reasons later to be discovered, traveling through the Fort DeSoto artesian well caused JJ, Isabella, and Zeke to flash back in time. Prehistoric Florida looked quite different than modern-day Florida, the trio would soon learn. They were transported to the end of the Ice Age period when glaciers at the polar caps were still melting, causing the oceans to rise up around the peninsula of Florida. The rising water nearly swallowed Florida whole. By the end of this great melting period, the Gulf of Mexico would be 100 feet deeper, and the distance between Florida's Gulf and Atlantic coasts would be shortened by 200 miles. The trio did not know they were thousands of years away from modern shipping ports, crowded cities, highways, and towering high-rise condominiums.*

The expansive view outside the cave opening diverted the trio's attention from finding their classmates on Mr. Celi's field trip. To the west, the tiny creek they had been following drained into a salt marsh that fed into the distant turquoise gulf. To the east, the landscape unfolded into alternating areas of pine forests and subtropical jungles. The tiny island where Ft. DeSoto once stood was dotted with small well springs. A herd of deer, some grazing on the grasses, others drinking from small well ponds, looked up at the Bayway Buccaneers in curiosity.

"I can't believe it," Isabella shook her head. "I've never seen deer at Fort De Soto before!"

"And have you also noticed?" Focusing the binoculars, JJ scanned the water. "There's no sign of civilization."

"Yeah, Toto! We're not in Kansas anymore!" Zeke laughed nervously, disguising his fear. "Where do you think we are?"

"I think we've time-traveled. Those cave drawings back there. They were real," JJ announced. "Just had a feeling!"

"You're off the chain, JJ. Get serious. There just has to be a good explanation for all this." Isabella searched her brain for a logical explanation. "Maybe they've cleared the island for a Disney movie?"

"No. Can't you see?" JJ pulled out his binoculars. "Somehow we've traveled back in time. Through some sort of porthole. Back to another era in Florida history. The cave drawings. And the bayway islands. Well, they haven't looked like this in thousands of years!"

"Your imagination is running again," Zeke said. "And now you're trying to suck us into your way of thinking. I agree with Izzy. There has to be another explanation."

Wooooosh! Wooooosh! Whoosh! A flurry of spears flew across the pine forest toward the grazing deer.

Thump! Thump! Thump! One by one, the small deer fell. The animals, arrows piercing their sides, lay dying on the grassy surface. One deer with huge horns, fell into a pond, its blood creating a red tide pool. The remaining animals scattered into the dense pine forest. When silence came, the hunters made their way toward the dying animals.

"I can't believe it." Isabella rubbed her eyes, then blinked. "They're cavemen, aren't they?"

"Or maybe early Native American Indians," JJ whispered, his voice trembling. "Now do you believe me? There is no other explanation. This is real."

"Oh, gawd..." Zeke's legs felt weak. "This can't be happening."

The Bayway Buccaneers hid still behind a palmetto thicket near the cave opening. They watched the Native Indians, a tribe of two dozen hunters, skin the deer and drag the carcasses into the Sand Pine forest.

"Sorry guys," Zeke' trembled with fear. "all of a sudden I feel a chill running down my spine. Let's get out of here. Let's go back in the cave."

"It'll be okay. We'll find our way back." Isabella comforted Zeke with a hug. "But I just don't get it? There has to be another explanation..."

"Look around," JJ whispered, handing the binoculars to Isabella. "Do you see any sign of civilization? Fort DeSoto? It's not here anymore! The Skyway Bridge? Gone! Do you see any houses on Anna Maria Island? It's not...."

15

"Okay! Okay! I get your point." Isabella waved her hand in the air. "But I still think there has to be another explanation!"

"I want to go back." Zeke's brown eyes grew wider as he listened to the conversation. "I got a bad feeling about all this. Let's go back through the cave..."

"Come on." JJ patted him on the back. "Where's your sense of adventure? Besides, we can't..."

"I want to go back, too." Isabella wrapped her arm around Zeke. "But how? We don't even know where we are!"

"I already told you." JJ slapped his forehead in frustration. "We're somewhere back in time."

Isabella closed her eyes a moment, trying to ignore JJ. Then, opening her eyes, she said, "Suppose you're right, JJ. That we've somehow time-traveled." Hearing her own words, Isabella shook her head in disbelief. "How do we get back home?"

"I don't know." JJ rubbed the coin in his pocket. "But everything seemed to have started when I found this gold..."

Wooosh! Whoosh! Whoosh! The sound of the hunters, following the herd of animals, was getting closer. The Bayway Buccaneers turned toward the distant sound.

"Boys, I don't know if that coin has anything to do with us being here," Isabella paused to scan the dense foliage for an escape route, "but we gotta do something. We can't wait around here. If those Indians, or whoever they are, find us there's no telling what they'll do to us."

"Hey, look. I just saw a light over there." Zeke pointed toward an island in the Gulf of Mexico. "Someone's signaling us."

"No. It's even better than that," Isabella said excitedly. "It's the Egmont Key lighthouse."

"You're right, Izzy," JJ agreed, training his binoculars on the lighthouse beacon. "Hey! And it looks like that ship again!"

"What ship?" Isabella and Zeke asked in unison.

"Back on the *Foul Belle*.." He focused the binoculars on the *GhostRider*. "As we approached the Fort DeSoto dock I saw that same ship anchored out on the Gulf. Now it's sailing through the passage near the old lighthouse. Can you make out the name?"

Zeke took a hard look, then passed the binoculars to Isabella. "Too far to see."

"I can't read it either," Isabella shook her head. "Are you sure it's the same ship?"

JJ took his binoculars back to take another look. "It sure looks like that Spanish galleon."

"We'll have to keep a close watch on that ship. Now, getting back to the lighthouse," Isabella unfolded Mr. Celi's *Letter of Marque*. Ignoring the mystery clues, she turned the letter over to the map. Placing her finger on Fort DeSoto, she dragged it along the edge of Mullet Key toward the Egmont Lighthouse. She tapped the paper with her index finger. "Look! This is Mullet Key where Fort DeSoto is..."

"Or was," JJ smiled.

"Or was," Isabella continued. "I think this is where we are, where we came out of the cave. And this is where the lighthouse is."

"If that's a map of the islands," Zeke shook his head. "How do you explain all this." He waved his arms as if performing a magic trick. "No bridge. No fort. No cities. This looks nothing like the bayway islands!"

"I don't know," JJ shrugged his shoulders. "But Izzy's right."

Isabella nodded. "It does match..."

"Hey, you know what?" JJ interrupted. "That map does show the islands..."

Zeke and Isabella exchanged bewildered glances.

"Just for a moment, let's say I'm right. That we traveled back in time." JJ's mind raced with electricity. "Then the map would not have yet been drawn. Not for thousands of years..."

"You're crazy, JJ!" Zeke waved his hand, dismissing JJ's words.

"Maybe so," JJ agreed. "Izzy, when was our map published?"

She took a closer look at the map key. "Two years ago, in 2002. But I'm not sure I follow you."

"Me neither," Zeke's brown eyes turned to Isabella. "He's totally lost me, too."

"Evolution and hurricanes, and other natural disasters. They would have changed the way Florida looked throughout the years." JJ shook his head. "And in our year, 2004, modern technology reshaped the looks of Florida's coastline. We've built tall condos and bridges. Cut down trees. Cleared beaches. So it stands to good reason that 21st Century Florida would look totally different. I'd say we're somewhere between prehistoric Florida and 16th Century Florida..."

"Gee, that narrows it down," Isabella answered sarcastically. "But why the 16th Century? Why not the 17th or 18th..."

"Or even the 19th Century?" Zeke interrupted.

"The doubloon," JJ pulled it from his pocket. "It's dated 1528. So we must be somewhere in the 16th Century..."

"I suppose that sorta makes sense," Isabella nodded, still puzzled. "At least I think it does. JJ, does your book say anything about old coins?"

"My *Florida Field Guide To Naval History?*" He shook his head. "I checked it already. It has a small chapter on Spanish doubloons, but it doesn't show any coin looking like this one."

"But how do you explain those prehistoric cave hunters?" Isabella shrugged. "They weren't around in the 1500's."

"And the lighthouse," Zeke pointed to Egmont Key. "How do you explain that? I know the Egmont lighthouse wasn't built in the 16th Century."

"Okay. I know we're in some sort of time warp. But I haven't figured that out. At least not yet," He paused, then raising a magic finger, JJ proclaimed, "but I think if we can somehow get across the water to Egmont Key where the lighthouse is..."

"It's our way back, isn't it?" Zeke interrupted. "It's about our only hope of getting back home."

"So we're all in agreement." Isabella folded the letter into her back pocket. "Somehow we'll have to avoid the Indians, and that ship. Then figure out a way to cross the passage to Egmont Key."

Chapter Seven

Tails The Trail

They followed the creek bed along a deer path, past the ponds and salt marshes. Determined to avoid the Indians, the Bayway Buccaneers chose to hike the thick vegetation rather than risk the open beach. They remained silent during much of the hike, occasionally stopping for a rest.

"Those sounds," Zeke rested on a downed pine. "they're giving me the jitters. Let's go back home through the cave..."

"Nothing to worry about," JJ assured him, wiping the sweat from his brow.

"Yeah." Isabella looked at JJ. Her blue eyes betraying the words she had just spoken. "Those sounds are. so far away."

Continuing down the deer path deeper into the forest, they reached a fork in the sandy trail. The creek trail seemed to lead to the south, toward the beach and Gulf. The other path led deeper into the dense pine forest.

"Now what?" Zeke looked up, hoping for divine intervention.

"Is the map of any help?" JJ asked. "Which way do you think is safer?"

Isabella pulled the map from her pocket and studied it. "The trails are obviously not on the map. But I think we're here. And both lead west toward the point on Mullet Key."

"And closer to Egmont Key," Zeke smiled, his white teeth flashing brightly.

JJ pulled the doubloon out of his pocket, rolled it in his fingers. "If it lands *ship side* up, we follow the creek trail toward the beach. Everybody *agrees?"*

"Sounds fair enough," Zeke nodded in agreement.

"Izzy," JJ handed the coin to Isabella, gave her a gentle smile. "You do the honors."

She flipped the coin. It went spinning in the air, end-over-end, landing in the soft sand.

"Yo Creo," JJ announced, as he stepped into a beam of sunlight spilling through the pines. "Looks like we take the forest trail."

****

𝓘𝓽 was late morning when the Bayway Buccaneers broke for lunch. Their appetites, spurned by the long hike along the sandy trail, were begging to be fed. JJ pulled a peanut butter and banana sandwich out of his knapsack. He gave half of it to Isabella. In exchange, she gave him blueberry pudding in a small plastic cup. Zeke sat in the shade of a scrub oak, barely touching his lunch.

"I'm not sure we made the right choice back at the fork." Zeke nibbled at a corn chip.

"What are you talking about?" JJ scooped a plastic spoon inside the pudding cup. He took a bite, then turned a page in his book. "Glad we chose boxed lunches today."

"Can't imagine what we would have done without our lunches." Isabella flicked the banana slice off her sandwich.

"I'm not even sure that's a good map we're following," Zeke said doubtfully. "And the light." He pointed toward the lighthouse. "We're not even sure what it is!"

"Look, Zeke. There are a lot of things we can't explain right now." JJ paused to turn the page in his field guide. "I don't know how we got here. Don't even know why we're here. But somehow we've traveled backwards. And that lighthouse is our only hope. It's our future. I have this feeling." He patted Zeke on the back. "We get to it, and we're home free."

"You and your feelings," Zeke shook his head, and gave a faint laugh. "They're really hurting mine." He removed the *Florida Gator* cap from his head, fanning his face. "Whew! Have you noticed it's gotten a lot hotter?"

"Yeah. It does seem quite hot for February." Isabella carefully balanced the juice carton and the open map on her bare legs. She sipped her juice, then gave a big smile. "I hope your feelings are right, JJ. Except for the unexplainable, everything makes sense!"

"May I quote you on that?" Zeke joked.

The Bayway Buccaneers allowed themselves a good laugh.

****

Lunch over, the Bayway Buccaneers continued down the forested sandy trail on Mullet Key. Pine and palm trees lined the path, with a few palmetto bushes scattered around. The strobes of light flashing from across the water and through the pines confirmed they were moving closer to Egmont Key.

"Look at that." JJ stopped on the sandy trail. "It's huge!"

"It's just a pile of shells," Zeke said, disinterestedly.

"No. It's a shell mound where Florida Indians used to pile all their old shells. I remember there used to be a shell midden back on Tierra Verde. Until the developers destroyed it." He removed the purple Hilfiger sweat shirt tied around his waste, then bunched it in the knapsack. "Geez, it's getting even hotter."

They continued hiking the narrow trail. The pines gave way to palm trees and palmettos. The pine needle bed gave way to sand and sand spurs.

"There's another one," Isabella pointed. "They're all over the place!"

"What's the big deal?" Zeke shifted his leather satchel to his left shoulder. "They're only shells!"

"Shhhhh. We need to keep our voices down," JJ said in a low voice. "The big deal is that we're walking though Indian territory."

"Caloosa Indians?" Isabella gave him a worried look. "They lived on the Bayway Islands."

"Maybe. Or the Tocobagas." JJ answered seriously. "Both lived on the Bayway Islands. But looking at those Indians back there, my guess is we're walking through sacred Tocobagan burial grounds."

"Oh, gawd....." Zeke's voice faded. His body went limp, falling face first into the sandy earth.

JJ turned Zeke over on his back. Isabella found a wide palmetto leaf and waved it back and forth in front of Zeke's face.

"You sure you're okay?" Isabella carefully plucked a sand spur from his hair.

"Yeah, I'm fine. Ouch!" Zeke pulled a sand spur from his eyebrow. He worked his way down his body, starting with his head. "Just a little embarrassed. Ouch!"

"You've been out for a while," JJ said with clear concern. "You had us

21

scared!"

"We did it again. Didn't we?" Zeke asked, climbing to his feet. It was more a statement than question. "We've time traveled again."

"Yeah. I suppose that does explain the weather change." Isabella held Zeke steady with one hand. "It does feel more like spring than winter."

"While you were laid out on the ground..." JJ opened his *Field Guide* to the chapter on *Early Naval Exploration*. "If those Tocobagan shell middens are real..."

"Slow down. Slow down." Zeke grabbed his notepad and pen. "I want to take this down. Might be some good material for my story."

"Well the good news is that..." Isabella searched for optimism in her voice, "if those shell middens are real, we're traveling forward in time...."

"Oh, no." Zeke scribbled a note. "Here comes the bad news. Right?"

"Yes. The bad news is..." JJ tapped the open *Field Guide* with his index finger, "we're still 500, maybe even a thousand years from home..."

"Oh, gawd!" Zeke wobbled on his feet.

"But..." Isabella fanned the palmetto leaf faster. She forced a smile. "But we are moving forward..."

"Oh, gawd!" Zeke fell limp a second time. "Oh, gawd."

Thump!

Chapter Eight

The Spanish Fleet
(1528)

After reviving Zeke a second time, the Bayway Buccaneers followed the Tocobagan trail through the palmettos. The trail led to a white beach on Mullet Key Point. Two palm tree heads lined the trail entrance, leading to an opening of blue skies and a calm Gulf of Mexico. Sunlight cut through the clear turquoise water and ivory sand bottom.

Zeke carefully ducked onto the beach. He looked left, then right. "No sign of the Tocobagans."

"Good." JJ followed Zeke. He found shade under a coconut palm. "Wonder where they could be? Haven't seen the Indians since we left the cave."

"I'm not sure if I care. Just as long as they're not here." Isabella wiped her brow with a forearm. She gathered her long blonde hair and tied it into a pony tail with a scrunchy. "Whew. Sure is getting hot."

"Gotta be at least 85 degrees out," JJ said, swatting a horsefly from his face. "Maybe even 90."

"Yeah." JJ sat down, leaned his back against the palm. He pulled the *Field Guide* from his knapsack, opening it again to the chapter on *Early Naval Exploration*. "Mind if I have a look at the letter?"

She removed the *Letter of Marque* from her pocket. "Here you are." Isabella handed him the letter.

"I don't know about you guys..." Zeke threw off his red Billagong T-Shirt and shoes. "But I'm getting in. It's time for another break."

"Be careful," Isabella called out. She removed a small stuffed bear from the top of her backpack, pulled out a towel and lotion, then returned the bear to the bag.

Splash!

Isabella placed her towel in the sun. "I wonder what Mr. Celi and the other kids are doing now? I'll bet they're worried about us!" Isabella wiped 50 spf sun block on her face and shoulders. "Want some?"

"No thanks." JJ peeled off his shirt, revealing his thin, but muscular body.

"You okay?" Isabella softly touched JJ's hand. "You seem so distant. You worried about something?"

He traced the map with his index finger. "I'm okay. But I'm sure Mr. Celi's doesn't even know we're missing."

"Why doesn't Mr. Celi like you?" She spread lotion on her long legs. "He never seems to believe anything you say."

"I suppose he has his reasons." He continued reading the map and field guide, then changed the subject. "The way I figure it..."

"Would you mind spreading some lotion on my shoulders?" Isabella smiled. She removed her pink T-shirt, then turned her back to JJ. "I tend to get sunburned if I'm not careful."

"Nice bathing suit, Izzy.." He massaged lotion on her white shoulders. "I love the turquoise color."

"Thanks." Isabella smiled. "I thought you'd like it."

"The way I figure it, Izzy, we're on Mullet Key Point. That means we're on the very spot where someday.." he tapped on the map, "...Fort DeSoto will be built right here. Someday it'll be facing the lighthouse over there."

"But how do we get across to Egmont Key?" Isabella asked, a trace of concern in her voice.

"Hey, come on in!" Zeke shouted, his voice nearly drowned by the warm breeze and surf. "Water's great!"

Isabella and JJ ignored him.

"Back there, right after we passed the oyster shell midden," JJ paused to gather his thoughts. "I didn't want to say anything because Zeke was already scared. Did you see the dirt mounds behind the palmettos?"

"Sure. I saw some mounds," Isabella laid on the towel. "What are you getting at?"

"Did you also see those crosses on some of the mounds? They were freshly dug. They weren't shell mounds." JJ became dead serious. "The Tocobagans never buried their dead that way. I think it was also a Spanish

24

graveyard! One of the crosses had a date on it, *1528*."

"Is that what's worrying you?" Isabella squeezed his hand.

"According to the field guide, the Tocobagans lived in this area for more than 700 years. When the Spanish explorers arrived in this area they slaughtered the Indians."

"Hey guys!" Zeke shouted. Now waist deep in the turquoise water, he stood 20 yards out on a sandbar. "Look!"

JJ and Isabella looked up at the sound of Zeke's voice.

"Ships!" Zeke hollered out as he rushed to shore. "Tall ones!"

JJ retrieved his binoculars and scanned the horizon toward the late afternoon sun. He counted three Spanish galleons, and a handful of smaller ships. Spanish soldiers, some wearing armored breast plates and helmets, watched chained Africans unload barrels and crates onto smaller longboats. The silver armor reflected the light off of the setting sun. JJ followed the fully loaded longboats paddling toward the south beach of Mullet Key.

"Guys," JJ's voice quivered. "Get off the beach. We're in big trouble."

The pirate beads clacked around their necks as the Bayway Buccaneers grabbed their belongings and hurried behind a palm tree head.

"Now what?" Zeke's brown eyes grew large. "What do we do now?"

"I don't know." JJ stared through the binoculars between the palm leafs.

"Do you think it's the same ship we saw earlier?" Isabella shifted her weight in the sand.

"I don't think so. Looks like they're flying under the Spanish flag." JJ trained the binoculars on the masts of the Spanish ships. "The one I saw was a pirate ship."

Zeke grabbed a towel to dry off. "But I thought you said it was a Spanish...."

"It was a Spanish galleon." JJ shook his head. "But the one I saw was crewed by pirates..."

"What do you mean?" Isabella snapped her head toward JJ. "Pirates? How can you be so sure?"

"Yeah." JJ nodded. "Didn't want to say anything before. But it had a *Jolie Rouge* flag..."

"A what?" Isabella asked.

"A *Jolie Rouge* flag." JJ returned the binoculars to his knapsack. "You know a jolly roger flag. The kind pirates always use in the movies? With cross bones and a skull..."

"Oh, boy," Zeke whimpered.

"Maybe we ought to take a closer look!" JJ suggested. "Maybe even try to talk to them? I just have this feeling..."

"You kidding?" Isabella waved a frantic gesture with her arms. "You just said we're in *big trouble*. Now you're suggesting we talk to them? This is no time for your school boy adventures. We ought hike away from them. That's what we should do." She paused to catch her breath. "Those soldiers look mean!"

"I think so too. They have whips, too!" Zeke added. "And did you see how they chained those slaves? I don't want to be one of them!"

"We gotta do something!" JJ turned down the trail. "You guys stay here while I have a look. Maybe I can get a hold of one of their longboats. We need a boat to get across to Egmont Key. Maybe this is our big break."

"It's a stupid idea, JJ." Isabella shook her head, disgusted. "But you're not going alone. I'll go with you."

"You kidding?" Zeke rushed to catch up. "You're not leaving me here alone."

Chapter Nine

Panfilo De Narvaez

The exploration of the Americas began when in 1492, Christopher Columbus accidentally sailed into today's West Indies. Columbus' discovery of the New World brought Ponce de Leon to La Florida 21 years later. But it was Spanish Captain Panfilo De Narvaez, the Bayway Buccaneers would learn later, who explored the Tampa Bay area. Narvaez's fleet of men, women, and countless slaves, would launch an expedition to explore Florida's Gulf Coastal region.

Forgetting about the gold coin and *Letter of Marque*, Isabella and Zeke followed in JJ's wake as he backtracked along the Tocobagan trail. Skulking to get a better look, they noticed the soldiers had taken over the village they passed earlier in the day. There was still no sign of the Tocobagans.

"Panfilo," asked one of the Spanish officers, *"is this land what you expected?"* The two officers sat at a campfire while the other soldiers and slaves unloaded the longboats. *"The heat is miserable. The bugs. They're torturing our men. And for what, Panfilo?*

"What are they saying, Izzy?" JJ was impatient. "You're taking Spanish class!"

"Shhh. Keep your voice down!" Isabella whispered back, trying to decipher the conversation. "I dropped out of *Spanish 1*. Remember?"

"Zeke," JJ reached in his knapsack for his field guide. "know any Spanish?"

"You're incredible, JJ." Zeke finished getting dressed. He rolled up his socks, then put his tennis shoes on. He tied them, then adjusted the ball cap on his head. "My family's from Africa. You're the one who's Hispanic. You should know what their saying..."

"I may be a Lopez, but I was never taught a word of Spanish." His face turned sad. "Besides, I never even knew my parents...You know that!"

"I'm sorry for bringing it up again..." Zeke patted him on the back. "Real sorry."

"Listen," Isabella changed the subject. "Maybe we can figure out what they're saying..."

"There's much to be learned here," Panfilo replied. "We are making history for mother Spain. Ponce De Leon, Columbus. Their time has come and gone. Others may follow...." He took a long excited pause. "This is our time. We've discovered tierra verde. A deep water port. Soon we may even find gold!"

"Anyone get that?" JJ asked anxiously, leafing through the chapter on Spanish Exploration In Florida.

"He said something about the fertile green earth here." Isabella brushed a blonde curl from her face. "And something about oro."

"Oro. What's that?" Zeke asked.

"They're searching for gold." JJ said excitedly. "Oro means gold, doesn't it?"

"Yeah," Isabella replied. "I think so. And that soldier on the left. He keeps calling the other one Captain Panfilo.... "

"Awesome," JJ interrupted. "I think that's Narvaez!"

"What...?" Zeke peeked through the palmetto brush at the officers.

"Narvaez?" Isabella whispered.

"Don't you guys remember anything Mr. Celi taught us?" JJ shook his head. "Panfilo De Narvaez was the first European to explore this area." He read the pages of his Field Guide. "Look. It says here that Narvaez and more than 600 soldiers..."

"600 soldiers...?" Isabella frowned.

"And countless slaves," JJ continued reading. "His exploration possibly brought the second group of slaves to arrive in North America..."

"Slaves?" Zeke closed his eyes, rubbing them. "Countless slaves..."

"They never found the gold they were looking for..." JJ angrily slapped the guide shut, making a loud cracking sound. "...But they terrorized and killed the Indians in this area."

"Did you hear that noise?" asked the young officer.

"Probably just a whip." Panfilo De Narvaez dismissed the question. "...A disobedient slave needs to know who's in charge. Have you heard from Lieutenant

Caraballo and his men..?"

"Shhhh." Isabella admonished JJ. "They'll hear us."

"Sorry. It just makes me mad." He reopened the book. "That was on April 15, 1528..."

"Oh, gawd," Zeke said wearily. "I'm feeling dizzy again."

"Come on, Zeke." JJ grabbed his elbow and lowered him to the ground. "Get a grip, will you?"

"Boys," Isabella interrupted. "Listen. They're saying something else."

"Yes, Captain." The Spanish officer removed a report from his breast pocket. "Lieutenant Caraballa is still searching for a deep water harbor. Just as you ordered. But..." the officer hesitated.

"But what?" Captain De Narvaez stood up. "Answer me."

"One ship is believed to have wrecked in last month's storm. And another ship, captained by Juan Jon..." the officer paused.

"What?" Narvaez interrupted. "What is it?"

"He and his crew...Well there are rumors that he and his crew..." he shook his head, disbelieving. "they may have mutinied..."

"That's impossible!" Captain De Narvaez shook his head. "Juan Jon would never abandon the mission. He is one of my best officers..."

"Sir," the lieutenant interrupted. "His ship has been missing since our arrival on La Florida."

"But why?" Narvaez wiped the sand off his black boot, then the other. "Why would Juan Jon do such a thing?"

"Of course," the lieutenant chose his words carefully, "it is only a rumor. But it may have something to do with the Tocobagans..."

"The Indians in this village are no longer a threat." Narvaez angrily pointed to the large mounds of dirt scattered around the villages. "And the other Tocobagans...if they cause us problems, they will suffer the same fate..."

"Excuse me, gentlemen," an armored soldier interrupted the conversation. His metal armor clanged to the rhythm of his abrupt pace. "Captain Narvaez..."

"Yes, Sergeant?" De Narvaez answered. "What is it?"

"The men are assembled for the ceremony," the sergeant replied.

****

The Bayway Buccaneers kept a safe distance as they followed Captain Panfilo De Narvaez and his men from the Indian village to the white sandy shoreline of the bay. A cluster of officers, in full armor, stood stiffly at attention. The other soldiers, facing each other, formed two parallel lines as Narvaez rode his horse between them.

Captain De Narvaez, now dressed in full armor, halted his horse short of the shoreline and the lapping bay waters. The setting sun colored the evening sky, and reflected a palette of orange and blue colors on Narvaez's armor. He dismounted and removed his silver helmet. Then, taking one step closer toward the bay, he dropped to his knees. With one knee in the sand, and the other in the gentle lapping surf, Narvaez proclaimed:

"We will soon travel northward in search of gold for the king. We know not what dangers we may face. But whatever they might be, we believe our journey is righteous." De Narvaez removed the sword from his sheath. He tapped the blade in the sand, then tapped it in the water. "Tonight, on behalf of King Charles I of Spain, I name these waters 'The Bay of the Cross.'"

De Narvaez paused, then whispered, "Yo Creo."

A light shone on the horizon from a distant island. It flickered in the darkening sky, reflecting on the glassy waters of the Gulf of Mexico.

Chapter Ten

Bunce's Pass

Hoping to put distance between them and Captain de Narvaez' fleet, the Bayway Buccaneers left the ceremony early. They headed west toward the point and the lighthouse, then northward to the end of the island. As the evening grew darker, it became more difficult to see through the thick palmetto vegetation. The trail ended at a narrow pass between Mullet Key and another island.

"Time to regroup," Zeke announced, plopping his body in the white sand. "Time for another break."

Isabella unfolded the *Letter of Marque* from her pocket. JJ knelt behind her, shining his penlight on the map in Isabella's hands. The late evening stars shone brightly on the trio as they took their brief respite on North Beach.

"Bunce's Pass," JJ pointed on the map. "I think that's where we are!"

"Sure looks like it," Isabella nodded. "So the island across is Shell Key. From what I remember, Bunce's Pass is deeper. This seems too shallow. We could almost walk across it..."

"...Not quite." JJ looked up from the map. "At least not yet."

"Look at those stars." Zeke, his hands behind his head, lay on his back watching the midnight sky. "It's so beautiful. Don't you think?"

"Yeah, beautiful." Isabella and JJ glanced upward, then resumed their conversation.

"Fast forwarding to the 21st Century." JJ turned his attention back to the pass. *"Bunce's Pass is deeper. Wider, too! But no telling how many tropical storms and hurricanes have blown through here since the 16th Century."*

"Yeah." Isabella agreed. *"One big storm and everything changes!"*

"But if this is Bunce's Pass.." Isabella sighed.

"...then we've been traveling away from the Egmont Lighthouse all evening!" Zeke shouted. He sat up from his prone position. *"We've been going the wrong way! I just knew it."*

"Chill out, Zeke." JJ answered defensively. *"We had no choice. We decided together that it was too dangerous to steal a longboat from..."*

"He's right." Isabella interrupted. She turned to Zeke. *"We had to get away from Narvaez' men. And heading this direction was our only option."*

"So what do we do now?" Zeke pleaded.

"It seems safer on the other island," Isabella responded. *"Don't you think?"*

"Yeah. And it looks like the tide is going out." JJ studied the current. *"I say we wait. In a an hour or so it'll be low tide. Then we can wade across the pass and find a place to camp."*

The trio waited for the tide to fall before crossing Bunce's Pass. But in making the crossing, it led them further away from the lighthouse, and their only beacon of hope...

Chapter Eleven

Making Camp

When an hour passed, the trio crossed the cool waters of Bunce's Pass. The outgoing current was strong, but the water was shallow enough to wade across the short distance between Mullet Key and Shell Island. They found a spot beneath a canopy of Sand Pines on a tiny spit of land. The Gulf bordered one side of their camp, and the bay bordered the other. The bed of pine needles at their feet cushioned the sandy earth below them. Isabella cleared the campsite while the boys searched the sparse pine forest for dry firewood.

While combing the woods, JJ found a flat rock. *Just what I was looking for,* he thought. He examined the smooth rock, then placed it in the pocket with the gold doubloon.

By the time the boys returned, Isabella had the campsite ready.

"Dinner for three," Isabella curtsied, then laughed. "I hope you boys brought home the bacon."

In their absence, Isabella had dug a fire pit, cleared twenty feet of pine straw from the hole, then circled three large sitting logs nearby. With strips of cloth torn from a T-shirt, Isabella tied two beach towels together and hung them over a horizontal pine branch. She pegged the ends of the beach-towel tent with tiny sprigs of pine wood, then spread a third towel below the triangular tent for ground cover.

"Great job, Izzy." Zeke dumped a load of firewood next to the fire pit.

"Yeah." JJ exclaimed. "Great imagination."

33

"Thanks guys," Isabella said. "Never knew my Girl Scout skills would come in so handy!"

"Good job on the tent." JJ walked toward the triangular-shaped tent. He pointed to a colorful towel with a large gecko sporting sunglasses. "I especially like this one. The lizard seems quite happy to be here."

"Oh, that towel?" Isabella laughed.. "I purposely faced the *Caribbean Soul* logo toward the campsite. I was hoping you'd notice it."

"But how did you tie...?" JJ took a second look. "Hey Izzy...You didn't tear up my favorite Buffett shirt...?"

"Nah." Isabella smiled. "It's one of my old shirts. Just went in your knapsack to check for food."

Zeke laughed, adjusting his *Gator* cap. "You and your fixation with all this nautical stuff..."

"Guys," Isabella laughed, then gave a worried look. "I took an inventory while you were gone. We only have enough snacks to last a day or so. If we're real careful...our juice packets will last a little longer..."

"Don't worry," JJ smiled. "We'll be walking the beach on Egmont Key by noon tomorrow."

"Yeah. I hope you're right," Zeke gave a worried laugh. "I hear starving to death is no picnic..."

"Glad you're keeping your sense of humor, Ezekiel," JJ smiled. "Don't worry, there's plenty of food on this island. We'll just have to catch it if we have to..."

Zeke placed some tree moss and kindling wood inside the sandpit, then laid some dried limbs on top. "It's ready, JJ."

"Do you really think we need that fire?" Isabella asked. "Narvaez and his men. They'll see us!"

"It'll get cold a little later," JJ said confidently. "We'll need the warmth, especially with our wet clothes. Besides, the smoldering moss will keep the bugs away, the light will be blocked by the trees, and the night will block any smoke from being seen."

"I love the way your mind works, JJ." Isabella hugged him. "You're always figuring things out."

"Thanks," JJ blushed. "If only I were right more often...."

"Come on, guys. Don't get all lovey-dovey on me." Zeke spread the couple apart, then turned to JJ. "How we gonna start the fire? Figure that one out, big guy," he said playfully.

"Flint." JJ smiled. He pulled the gold doubloon and flat rock out of his cargo shorts. He scraped the old coin against the rock. On the third try sparks flew from the edge of the coin and flint. The moss smoldered, and smoke rose through the sand pines and into the midnight sky. The kindling wood burned brightly. JJ tossed a log into the pit, fanned the fire with his Tampa Bay Buccaneers cap. The campfire roared to life. "Yo Creo," he whispered, returning the coin to his pocket.

Chapter Twelve

True Confessions

"This is sweet," JJ exclaimed. He sat on a log near the campsite examining the map on the *Letter of Marque*. He swallowed the final bite of a twinkie.

"What?" Zeke smiled. He jotted a note on his pad. The evening air cooled to a light chill, and he huddled near the warm fire. "You've never had a roasted twinkie before?"

"No." JJ shook his head, disbelieving. "This whole experience is sweet."

"Watcha writing, Zeke?" Isabella lay on the sand, her head cushioned against a log by a stuffed Teddy Bear. "You working on that story for the *Tidal Tales*? You surely have lots to write about..."

"I'm writing something else right now." Zeke clicked his pen closed. "Actually just finished my first poem..."

"Really?" Isabella smiled. "Now that's *sweet*! Mind if I read it?"

"You're writing poetry now?" JJ's face contorted.

"I think it's romantic." She turned to JJ. "You could take some lessons from Zeke."

"My romance is the adventure I find from the sea. She's all the romance I can handle..." JJ adjusted his position on the log. Then, giving Isabella a warm look, he added, "for right now..."

"No laughing, Izzy." Zeke handed the notepad to Isabella. "You too, JJ! I'm a real sensitive guy."

"*Maiden's Arrival, by Ezekiel*." Isabella looked up from the notepad.

"No last name?"

"Nah. Lots of really famous people use only one name." Zeke shrugged, then gave a laugh. "I figure I might as well get a jump-start on my writing career with a positive attitude..."

"Okay, guys. Let's get serious." Isabella tilted the pad toward the flickering campfire. She read Zeke's scribbled note:

"Maiden's Arrival, by Ezekiel

Drift slowly here,
Harbor your heart
Cast away your fears
May we never part

Attach me securely
Sail away never
Board me gently
And love me forever..."

"That's beautiful, Zeke." She hugged him. "You're going to be a famous writer someday."

"That was nice," JJ agreed. "But kinda mushy for my taste."

"I think he has a flair for writing romance." Isabella lay back down, adjusting the bear behind her head.

"I think adventure on the high seas can be kinda of romantic, don't you think?" JJ poked Isabella in the ribs. "The kids. And Mr. Celi. They'll never believe our adventures!"

"They're probably not even thinking about us." Zeke interjected. "I'll bet they snuck out again. Mr. Celi doesn't know it, but they're out somewhere breaking the law."

"Or maybe they're still trying to figure out the answers to those stupid mystery clues," JJ said sarcastically. He turned the *Letter of Marque* over to the clues, then quickly turned the letter back to the map side.

"Gee, JJ. You're really tough on Mr. Celi," Isabella said pointedly. "Don't you think he tries to make his classes interesting?"

"Yeah, I suppose you're right," JJ conceded, turning his eyes away.

Isabella turned a serious look to Zeke. "How'd you end up at the boarding school?"

"Actually, it's very simple. I hope to be a writer someday. I love the way

Ernest Hemingway and Pat Conroy write. But except for my English classes..." Zeke lifted his pad and pen in the air. "...I refused to do my other work in school. So after I failed eighth grade for the second time..."

"Twice?" Isabella asked. "I only failed once."

"Yeah, twice." Zeke gave an embarrassed laugh.

"That's why you're at the Bayway School?" Isabella asked curiously.

"Well, that and..." Zeke paused a moment. "I started my own underground newspaper..."

"You did?" Isabella smiled. "That's quite impressive!"

"I guess I crossed the line when I began writing humorous editorials. I made fun of everyone, including my teachers and the principal." Zeke shook his head. "All the kids thought it was funny. But the adults, well, sometimes they don't have a sense of humor. So my parents sent me away to the reform school. Actually, the change has done me good. The smaller school gave me a fresh start with writing at the *Tidal Tales Telegraph*. What about you, Izzy? Why did your parents send you to the boarding school?"

JJ turned away, staring at the gleaming Gulf through the pine trees. Abandoned as an infant, he knew nothing about his parents. And conversations about family always left him with deep-seated resentment. Invariably, the feelings of abandonment would chip away at his self confidence. In its worst form, it would turn to an emptiness that could only be satisfied by retreating deep inside himself.

But in that place within, JJ could imagine his life the way he wanted it to be. A place where he could be whom ever and where ever he wanted to be. Mostly, however, it was a safe harbor where he could safely ride out his personal storm. Isabella and Zeke's conversation, unknowingly, forced JJ to that dark place...

"I guess I still have ambitions of being a military officer someday..." Isabella turned on her side. "I fantasize about meeting Colin Powell some day...My mother thinks he's such a *hottie!*"

"Colin Powell? Who's he?" Zeke shook his head. "Never heard of him!"

"Really?" She gave him a puzzled look. "I think he's one of the greatest leaders of our time..."

"You're a great leader." Zeke stood up, pumping his fist in the air. "Isabella for President!"

"You're being silly," Isabella laughed. "Sit down before I..."

"No kidding." Zeke returned to his seat on the log. "You've got great integrity, and you're not bad to look at...."

"Thanks," Isabella blushed. "But after my father died..."

"I'm sorry, Izzy." Zeke gave her a sympathetic glance. "I didn't know..."

"It's okay," Isabella answered. "For a while I couldn't talk about it to anyone. Before Daddy died, he gave me this Teddy Bear. He goes everywhere with me..."

"I was wondering why that bear always tags along..." Zeke kicked the burning logs with his shoe.

"I know that I'm a little too old for stuffed bears, but the right time will come when I can give him up," Isabella smiled wistfully. "Anyway, a few years after Daddy died, my mother remarried. She gave my stepfather all the attention, and I felt so alone. So I did stuff to get my mom's attention. Skipped school. Got arrested. Then was kicked out of JROTC..."

"You? Queen Isabella?" Zeke mocked her. "Miss goody-two-shoes got arrested?"

"Twice actually. For truancy each time." She shook her head. "But the attention I got from my mom wasn't what I expected. I thought creating havoc would get things back the way they were before she remarried..."

"...Instead, you were sent to the boarding school?" Zeke interrupted. "Right?"

"Yeah, more or less," Isabella agreed. "But like you, being away has given me time to think. And it has gotten me closer to my mother."

Noticing for the first time that JJ had withdrawn from the conversation, Isabella reached her arm toward him. "You okay? You're so quiet..."

"...I'll be fine." JJ turned a sad face toward Isabella, then stoked the dying fire with a tree branch. "Just listening to your conversation makes me feel a little sad..."

Isabella squeezed his shoulder. "We can change the subject if..."

"No. It's okay." He warmed his hands on the open fire. "I was abandoned as a kid. You guys know I was raised in a foster home. Actually..." JJ corrected himself, "so many homes I can't even count them... Never knew my parents. Don't know the meaning of family. I don't even know if I have any brothers or sisters. I've never even seen my birth certificate so I don't even know what the letters in my name stand for! Maybe nothing?"

"Sorry, JJ," Zeke apologized. "We didn't mean to..."

"It's okay, really." He nodded his head. "I've got a lot of anger built up inside me..."

"You just gotta get mad," Isabella wagged a mocking finger at JJ. "Then get over it..."

"Yeah, I know," JJ agreed. "I just haven't gotten to that point yet...but I'm working on it!"

"When I get angry," Zeke waved his pen in the air. "I just put pen to paper and..."

"But I'm not a writer like you," JJ shrugged. "I can't express what I feel in poems. I try to escape reality through my pirate fantasies. But in the end, I still have to face the reality of my situation, and all the anger bottled inside..."

Isabella reached for JJ. She kissed him on the cheek. "I'm sorry."

"...Sometimes I stop believing in people," JJ said. He wiped the moisture from his eyes. "Even when I know they want to help me..."

"But you're so smart, JJ." Zeke patted him on the back. "You'll figure it all out."

"Thanks, Zeke. I needed to hear that." JJ smiled through bleary eyes. "Sometimes I don't know what, or who, to believe in. Not even myself anymore..."

"I've felt that way a lot." Isabella wiped her eyes. "Especially after my father died..."

"Yeah, me too," Zeke sniffled. "That it's me against the world..."

"But look how we've gotten ourselves out of this mess." Isabella forced a smile.

"So far," Zeke added.

"So far..." JJ sniffled, then gave a laugh. "But we still have a lot of years ahead of us."

"We'll get through this adventure. And you'll work through your angry feelings." She kissed JJ again. "I'm sure of it."

"Thanks. I always try to keep a positive attitude." JJ squeezed Isabella's hand. "My imagination and my attitude are what keep me going."

"You do have a great imagination," Zeke agreed. "Maybe you ought to be a writer, too!"

"Nah. But I am like you in one way." JJ turned to Zeke. "I only wanted to study one thing in school. But my subject was history. Just loved it. Since I couldn't be a pirate, I thought maybe I could be an archeologist someday. You know, dig up mysteries of the past..."

"Cool," Zeke encouraged him, "like *Indiana Jones!*

"Yeah, like Indy." JJ shook his head in disappointment. "But when my grades started falling in the other classes, well, I sort of gave up on my history studies too..."

"So you were sent to the Bayway School for failing..?" Zeke asked.

"Nah." He shook his head. "A lot of the families I lived with were good people. But the last family I was with. Well....just as long as I kept

40

out of trouble they didn't care how I did in school."

"So how did you end up at the boarding school?" Isabella twirled a long blonde curl with her finger.

"Like you," he turned to Zeke and smiled. "I was about to fail eighth grade for the second time. So..." he took a long pause. "You know those state FCAT tests?"

"Yeah. The ones we have to pass to graduate?" Zeke said.

"How could we forget those tests...?" Isabella nodded.

"Right. Well, I stole copies of those tests. Gave 'em out to my classmates." JJ shook his head. "Seemed like a good idea at the time. Thought we all could brush up on our studies before having to take the test!"

"So you're the one we read about in the *St. Pete Times*?" Zeke looked up from the dimming campfire.

"Yeah. It was a big scandal. But, because I was a minor they didn't release my name in the papers." JJ answered, embarrassed. "I'm the one. After my arrest I went to court. The judge gave me a choice..."

"Jail time," Isabella nodded, "or the boarding school."

"Right. But hey," JJ smiled. "I wouldn't have met you guys..."

"You're right." Isabella smiled. "We have each other now."

"Yeah," Zeke agreed. He moved toward the tent. "We're family."

A cool breeze blew through the sand pines, loosening the needles. Isabella brushed her windblown hair away from her face. She looked up at the falling pine needles.

"Looks like a storm's brewing," she said, glancing in the direction of Egmont Key. "I wonder how we'll get out to the lighthouse?"

"We're less than ten miles away," JJ assured her. "Home's right across that passage."

Isabella and JJ quietly walked toward the tent where Zeke lay silently.

"You have to admit, Izzy," JJ whispered. "it's been quite an experience so far...and nothing bad has happened!"

"So far. The lighthouse may be ten miles away," Isabella laid her head on the stuffed bear next to Zeke's feet, "but we still have nearly 500 years ahead of us."

"You're not scared, JJ?" Zeke asked. "Not even a little?"

"Maybe, but I'm more excited than scared." JJ removed his sandals, placing them neatly outside the tent. "We just need to keep a positive attitude."

"I'm sure you're right. And I don't think it's as bad as it seems." Isabella removed her socks, stuffing them deep inside the toes of her shoes. "It'll all look better in the morning. You'll see."

Zeke curled his body. "Good night, guys!"

"Night, Zeke," Isabella whispered. She lay her head down near Zeke's feet, then reached for JJ's hand. "Pleasant dreams, JJ."

"Good night, Izzy." He squeezed her hand. "Yo Creo."

Chapter Thirteen

The Great Gale
(1848)

The rush of wind broke the calm of morning, blowing the trio further from Panfilo De Narvaez, and closer to present-day Florida. The hurricane would push them away from Spanish *La Florida*, and into the middle of the 19th Century when the new state of Florida belonged to a struggling country called the *United States of America*. The trio had not yet discovered, however, the importance of the gold doubloon and how it related to the mystery clues hidden in Mr. Celi's *Letter of Marque*.

A high-pitched sound squealed across the Gulf of Mexico, through the sand pines on Shell Key, then across Tampa Bay. The wind vibrated the tree branches above the tent. Pine needles swirled in the air like a mini vortex. Palm fronds hurled across the campsite, then disappeared in the dark sky. The rain chased the strong gusts of wind, pelting the sides of the towel tent like wet bb's. Then silence came, and the calm of the morning was restored.

"Wake up! Wake up!"

"Damn!" JJ sat up in the tent, hitting his head on the supporting tree limb. He fell backwards. Then sat up a second time, hitting his head against the same tree branch. "Damn! I did it again."

"Stop your swearing, JJ." Her eyes still closed, Isabella sat up in the towel-tent. "What's going on?"

"Was that my imagination?" JJ rubbed the lump on his forehead, then slowly opened his eyes. He looked out at the campsite, then up toward the

43

black sky. "Nope. A big storm's been here. I think we're between squalls. Looks like another one will be here soon."

"Oh, gawd!" Zeke cried. "Does the adventure have to start so early in the morning?"

"What are we waiting for?" Isabella quickly exited the tent, carefully avoiding the overhead branch. "Let's pack up and get out of here!"

The Bayway Buccaneers dressed quickly, packed their bags, then broke camp. Electrified by both fear and a sense of adventure, they skulked their way down the open beach.

"You think Narvaez is still out there?" Zeke sat on a washed-up railroad tie to put on his socks and shoes. "You see anything?"

"Don't think so," JJ said, peering through the binoculars, noticing the flash of light from Egmont Key. "All the ships are gone!"

"Maybe they've found a safe harbor before the storm hit?" Isabella wondered. "Mind if I have a look?"

"According to the field guide, that was one of their missions." JJ handed her the binoculars. "To find a deep water port for future exploration."

"Maybe they discovered the Port of Tampa?" Zeke kicked the sand off his red tennis shoes. "Now wouldn't that be exciting?"

"I wonder if we're still in 1528?" Isabella scanned the Gulf of Mexico with the binoculars. "Do you think we did some time-traveling overnight?"

"I don't know," JJ shook his head, then adjusted his Buccaneer cap. "Why would you ask that?"

"Well, all the ships are gone," Isabella handed the binoculars to Zeke, then pointed toward the horizon. "except that one."

"Looks like a Spanish galleon." Zeke adjusted the binoculars. "I wonder if it's part of Narvaez's fleet?"

"Let me have a look." JJ took the binoculars, focusing on the ruffling flag on the tall ship. "It's flying the *Jolie Rouge*. It's the *GhostRider*, the pirate ship I first saw back at Fort DeSoto! That ship seems to be traveling alone..."

"I guess the *GhostRider* would be outgunned with Narvaez's fleet around." Isabella concluded.

"So do you think that means that Narvaez and his men are nowhere around these waters?" Zeke asked.

"Can't be sure," JJ nodded. "but probably so."

"My hat," Zeke shouted, running down the beach. A gust of wind lifted his *Gator* cap from his head, then blew it across the sand like a tumbleweed.

"Hell!" JJ looked up at the darkening sky. "Another squall's coming! Looks like it's going to be even bigger than the last one!"

"I told you to stop swearing." Isabella waved her finger at JJ. "I don't like that."

"*Hell* is not swearing," JJ insisted. "Not if you use it in the Biblical sense. And right about now all *hell* is going to break loose. We better gather up Zeke, then find some cover real fast!"

Chapter Fourteen

The Sherrod Edwards

Between storms, and no longer fearful of Narvaez and his fleet, the Bayway Buccaneers walked the beach northward along Shell Key. Searching for higher ground, they kept a watchful eye on the *GhostRider* and the dark, churning storms in the Gulf of Mexico. The trio worked their way toward the North Channel, dodging derelict crates and barrels washing up in the surf.

"Why do you think that ship isn't worried about finding a safe harbor?" Isabella asked, wiping away rain drops from her face.

"I don't know, but it seems rather foolish to me. There's no way a ship, even that size, could ever ride out this kinda storm." JJ pulled out a dry beach towel from his bag. "Here Izzy."

"I wonder where this stuff is coming from." Zeke spit rainwater from his lips. "Think one of the galleons wrecked out there?"

"Can't believe this is happening," Isabella gave a serious laugh. She wiped her face with JJ's towel, then pulled a mirror out of her book bag. "We're walking through the middle of a hurricane and I'm not dressed for it. I'm a mess. My hair looks like a dark mop topped with a red cherry scrunchy," she laughed.

"But remember," Zeke said half smiling at Isabella. "It was your *tomorrow's a new day* speech..."

"Well she did say today would *look* different." JJ rummaged through the litter on the beach. "And see what a good night's rest will get you.

Look at this stuff here!"

"Aren't you the least bit scared?" Isabella pleaded. "Look what the storm did to this Spanish galleon!"

"I'm not sure if this stuff is from the Spanish expedition!" JJ trained the binoculars toward North Channel. "Izzy may be right. We may have time-traveled. Last night, or maybe this morning."

"What do you mean?" Zeke asked, not sure he wanted to know the answer. "You trying to scare us again?"

"What makes you think that?" Isabella wrung water from her hair. "What makes you think we've moved closer to the future. I mean the present, *our present*?"

"I dunno," JJ said. "I just have this feeling. That storm came up on us so quickly. There was no sign of it coming before we went to sleep last night!"

"I suppose that makes sense," Isabella said.

"But it doesn't change our situation," Zeke added. "We still have to find higher ground before the eye of the storm really hits us hard!"

"Or a boat!" JJ shouted. "There's a boat up ahead. A real boat!"

JJ handed the binoculars to Zeke.

"It is a boat!" Zeke danced a jig in the white sand. "Must have washed up on shore from the storm!" He tossed the binoculars to Isabella.

"Can't see anything," she said, wiping the rain from the lenses. "There, that's better. It's an old wooden longboat. Has something written on the side. I think it says, *Sherrod Edwards*."

****

The wooden boat, although swamped on the beach with sand and water, was otherwise seaworthy. JJ and Zeke bailed the saltwater out with their ball caps, while Isabella scooped out the white sand with a flat piece of driftwood. While getting the longboat *ship-shape*, the Bayway Buccaneers argued their next course of action, concluding their choices were few: abandon the boat in search of higher ground; row the small boat toward

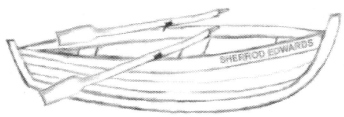

the lighthouse and into the raging storm; or head toward the mainland, and away from their only beacon of hope.

"Okay JJ, I suppose we have no other choice," Isabella conceded. "We'll take the longboat and row it toward Cabbage Key!" She paused thoughtfully. "If we make it that far. After the storm passes we'll head back toward Egmont Key...."

"I'm not sure about this, guys." Zeke disagreed, "I think we should find higher ground here on the island!"

"No time now," JJ said. "We gotta move fast! Besides there *is* no higher ground on Shell Key. You know that!"

"JJ's right," Isabella adjusted the strap on her book bag. "But first, let's try to salvage some of this stuff on the beach."

"Good idea, Izzy," JJ nodded, then smiled, "cause you never know..."

Chapter Fifteen

Playing Turtle

Waiting for a break in the weather, the trio dragged the *Sherrod Edwards* into the surf, then loaded the salvaged supplies. They rowed the wooden boat beyond the angry surf, where the water was deeper, but more calm. The longboat moved north, toward North Channel, and along the stormy shoreline of Shell Key. Then, turning eastward, they rowed away from the open waters of the Gulf of Mexico, and away from the driving wind and rain.

"Row," Isabella ordered. "Row. We gotta paddle together. The wind's picking up. We're running out of time."

"The good news is, the wind's at our back! It's pushing us closer to shore." JJ shouted above the howl of the wind. "The bad news is, the wind direction could change at any moment..."

"Thanks for the words of encouragement. That made my day!" Zeke said sarcastically. He looked over his shoulder, then said hopelessly, "The lighthouse. Can't see the beacon anymore. It's gone!"

The trio continued toward the higher ground on Cabbage Key, and into the relative safety of a mangrove lagoon. The storm grew more intense as the Bayway Buccaneers dragged the *Sherrod Edwards* up the embankment, then turned it upside down. Hurriedly, they tied the longboat between two Cabbage Palms, stashed their bags and supplies beneath its bow, then ducked under the hull.

"I guess we just wait." Isabella wiped mud from her cheeks. "Have a hurricane party and ride out the storm!"

"Izzy, can you reach my knapsack?" JJ held a small bottle in his hand. "I need my penlight."

"Can you get my bag, too?" Zeke asked. "I'd like to update my journal."

"Watcha have in your hand?" Isabella retrieved the three bags from the bow of the longboat. "Is that a bottle, JJ?"

"Yeah. I found it on the beach along with the other stuff." JJ reached in the bag for his penlight and field guide. "Wow! I forgot I had this. Here, have some beef jerky?"

"I'm not sure where I'm going with this," Zeke laughed, his mouth full of jerky. "But this story better make it to the front page of the *Tidal Tales Telegraph*."

"Here's an interesting fact you can use." JJ shined the penlight on the old bottle. "It's an old shaving lotion bottle. Has a stamp on it that says, *Made in USA*."

"So I was right. We have time-traveled." Isabella examined the clear bottle.

"Ouch! That stung." The hull of the *Sherrod Edwards* vibrated from the screaming wind. The boat lifted slightly, allowing rainwater to shoot upwards in Zeke's face. "I think the storm's getting worse."

"You're right." JJ grabbed onto the gunnels, then pulled down. He reached for his beach towel in the knapsack. "Grab your towels, guys. If we can keep the wind and rain from leaking in..." He stuffed the towel between the edge of the boat and the ground. "It'll form a vacuum. The wind and rain will blow right over us."

"Great idea," Zeke smiled, stuffing his towel in the opening. "I think it's working. The boat's not shifting as much."

"So you think we're no longer in *La Florida*?" Isabella rubbed the indented stamp on the clear bottle.

"I know we're somewhere after 1776..." JJ turned the pages on the Field Guide, "...but I can't really tell. It says here that the United States bought Florida from Spain in 1819!"

"Anything stamped on the stuff we salvaged?" Zeke asked, scribbling on his notepad. "Like maybe a date? Something like that?"

"Good idea!" Isabella squeezed his shoulder, then crawled toward the bow of the longboat.

"Here, Izzy," JJ handed the penlight to her. "You'll need this."

"Looks like all this stuff was on its way to Egmont Key before it was washed on shore." Isabella shined a beam of light on a small wooden box. "Look at the address, 'Light keeper, Egmont Key, Florida, USA'."

Zeke wrote *Egmont Key Lighthouse* on his notepad, then wrote the word *date*, followed by a question mark. "When was the lighthouse built?"

JJ flipped to the chapter on Florida lighthouses. "Izzy, would you shine the light here?"

Isabella and Zeke huddled around the light beam as JJ read from the guide.

"Here it is." JJ tapped the page. "It says the second Egmont Lighthouse was built in 1858. It was rebuilt after the first one was destroyed in a hurricane in what historians describe as *The Great Gale of 1848.*"

"Oh, gawd!" Zeke covered his eyes.

"'The hurricane ripped through Tampa Bay,'" JJ read. "'It tossed ships on the water like bath toys. A tidal surge flooded the bayway islands. When the tide receded, the rush of water destroyed many barrier islands. The surge also created new islands. Many historians believe the Gale of '48 was largely responsible for cutting Cabbage Key into two separate islands...'"

"Cabbage Key..." Isabella gave JJ a worried look. "that's the island we're on..."

"'...By the storm's end,'" JJ turned the page, "'the first Egmont Lighthouse, which once stood proudly at 87 feet above ground, was no longer standing.'"

"The boat's leaking," Zeke shouted, grabbing his leather satchel. Water's spilling in from underneath..."

The storm surge filled the longboat with churning tidewater. "I'm having a hard time breathing." Isabella choked back a mouthful of stinging saltwater.

"Hold your head up," JJ pushed Isabella's face upward toward the air bubble, "and breathe through your mouth..."

The storm raged for another hour. The tide repeatedly rose with a vengeance, then reluctantly returned to the sea. Rain and wind streaked between the gunnels and wet sand. The *Sherrod Edwards* shivered with every gust of wind. JJ, Isabella, and Zeke held firmly to one another.

"We're never going to survive this," Zeke said, choking back the salt water in his lungs. "If we don't...Just wanted you to know that a guy couldn't have any better friends than you two..."

"Thanks, Zeke. But we *are* going to make it. Just hold on and remain calm!" Isabella shouted. "Did you forget about our lucky coin?"

"Yeah, Izzy's right." JJ forced a laugh, tightening his grip on Isabella. "Besides, you still have your first book to write." He pulled the coin from the pocket of his cargo shorts, then squeezed it. "Think positively. We just have to keep believing..."

Chapter Sixteen

Billy Barefoot
(1861)

The light of a new day brought plenty of sunshine. The sunlight, however, was a stark contrast to the storm of the *Civil War* raging over the entire United States. The war began in 1861, and would last five long years. It would be one of America's darkest periods in history. It was a time when families from America's North and South, killed one another over the right to own slaves. Although they would meet under the cloud of war, the chance meeting between Billy Barefoot and the Bayway Buccaneers would cast a ray of hope for the future.

The *Sherrod Edwards* lay upside down, still anchored to broken Cabbage Palms. Mangrove trees, tattered and torn from an unsympathetic storm, lay on the beach next to broken palm branches and washed up sea grass.

"Ain't seen dis befo," said Azaelia, with a sweet southern drawl.

"Me neither," answered Victoria. "Maybe it blew in from last night's storm?"

"Shee-Rahhhhhd Edd-Waahds." Azaelia read the painted words on the wooden longboat. "Who's that, Grandpa Billy?"

"I recognize de name." The tall black man with a graying beard, spoke in a deep gravely voice. "Sherrod Edwards. Knew him, knew his brotha, Marvel, too. Sherrod was de old lighthouse keeper."

"Where do you think it came from, Mr. Billy?" Victoria moved cautiously around the boat. She wore her long dark hair loosely over her shoulder.

"Dunno! Cain't be da same Edwards, though," Billy Barefoot said. "Dey ain't been in dees parts for sometime!"

Billy Barefoot studied the longboat for a while, slowly circling it. He knocked on the hull and pawed at it as if he had discovered an alien spaceship.

****

The Bayway Buccaneers, still waterlogged, woke to the sound of soggy footsteps outside the *Sherrod Edwards*. Sunlight streaked below the gunnels, revealing three sets of feet surrounding the longboat. Scratching and knocking sounds vibrated from the wooden hull.

"What do you think we should do?" JJ whispered.

"Don't know," Zeke replied. "Got any ideas?"

"Shhhhh. Keep your voice down," Isabella whispered. "They'll hear us!"

"They're speaking English," Zeke said in a surprised voice.

"Maybe we're back home?" JJ uncurled his body beneath the hull of the boat.

"Maybe. Do you understand what they're saying?" Isabella asked.

"Not really. But we can't stay here all day," Zeke said softly. "They'll find us, sooner or later."

"Then who goes first?" JJ asked. "Who's going to be the guinea pig?"

"I will," Isabella said bravely.

"You sure?" JJ worried. "Maybe one of the guys should go out first?"

"One of us needs to go," Isabella insisted. "And I volunteered first. So I go!"

Bang! Bang! Bang! The deafening sound echoed inside the wooden hull.

"Som'body in der?" asked a gravely voice.

****

The hull of the *Sherrod Edwards* was right-sided, splashing the Bayway Buccaneers with blinding rays of sunshine. The warmth felt good. A large black hand, rough and weathered from working the farm fields, reached toward them.

"What you young'ns doin' in der?" Billy Barefoot questioned. "You wit de rebels?"

53

"No, sir," Isabella stammered. "We were just hiding from the hurricane..."

"Hurricane?" Victoria questioned. "There hasn't be one of those around here in quite some time."

"But the *Field Guide* says..." Zeke answered.

"Shhh."

"Name is Billy. Peoples, dey call me Billy Barefoot." He paused a moment. His kind dark eyes peered through his wrinkled face. "Dis is my granddaughter, Azaelia. And dis is her friend, Victoria."

"Hel..Hel.. Hello." The Bayway Buccaneers answered, reaching to shake their hands. They studied the dark faces of Billy and Azaelia. Their faces stood in contrast to Victoria's white complexion. "Nice to meet you!"

"Ain't from these parts, is you," Billy asked, more a statement than question.

Billy Barefoot helped the trio drag the longboat up to higher ground. At JJ's suggestion, they covered the boat with palm leaves for possible future use. Then, grabbing their bags and supplies, they followed Billy Barefoot and the two children down a subtropical path deep into the heart of Cabbage Key.

"I recognize that," Isabella smiled in amazement. "That's the old Tocobagan Indian mound on Tierra Verde...

"Yeah, I remember," Zeke pointed. "There used to be a big brown road sign next to it..."

"...until the developers got ahold of it," JJ completed his sentence. Then added angrily, "and wiped away any trace of the island's heritage."

"Ain't been any Indians in dees parts for quite some time," Billy corrected, shaking his head. "The Confederates, they is our concern, now!"

Along the way the trio explained to Billy Barefoot how it was they ended up hiding beneath the *Sherrod Edwards*. They told him about the *Letter of Marque*, the gold doubloon, Narvaez's fleet, the hurricane, and the Egmont Lighthouse.

"And the *GhostRider*. Almost forgot to mention the pirate ship." JJ slapped his forehead. "It seems to be following us."

"You sure?" Billy turned to JJ. "Ain't been pirates around neither. As I said, the rebels is our only concern now."

Chapter Seventeen

Little Victoria

The path led to a large campsite where several Negro families lived. Smoke billowed from the campfire, filling the air with an aroma of fatback and baked beans.

"Welcome to our home," Billy said proudly. "Got de tents from de rebels."

"Confederates didn't actually give 'em to us, mind you," Azaelia interjected proudly. "We stole 'em!"

Billy Barefoot played the perfect host. He cleared one of the tents for the Bayway Buccaneers. Billy gave them dry clothes to change into, and JJ, Isabella, and Zeke took turns changing, hanging their wet clothes on the line to dry. Later, at the campsite where a field kitchen was setup, he introduced the three teenagers to his family and friends.

"Billy says you ain't from here," one of them said.

"Well," JJ hesitated. "we are, and we aren't."

"Figured so," said the woman with an apron. "Could tell by the way you is dressed."

"From *Englund*?" asked a young black woman, a baby in her arms. "Ain't never seen dem kinda shoes and britches!"

"Or maybe from up *noth*?" Then, staring at Zeke, the aproned woman said, "Don't mean to be nosey or anythin', but you was wearing some fancy clothes for a colored boy!"

"Mind yer manners." Billy shot back. "Dees kids is our guests!"

55

"It's okay," Zeke answered. "We're just as surprised as you are about all this."

"Azaelia, darlin'," Billy gently placed a hand on his granddaughter's shoulder. "fetch these kids some coffee."

"Starbuck's, cafe mocha, please." Zeke joked.

No one laughed.

"Zeke," Isabella whispered, "stop it with your jokes!"

Billy turned to Victoria. "How 'bout serving our guests some dinner? I bet dey be real hungry."

Azaelia and Victoria went to the field kitchen to prepare dinner for their guests.

"They're best friends, aren't they?" Isabella watched the two young girls scoop dinner onto tin plates. "Seems like they get along real well."

"Dey been friends since dey was babies. And she," Billy nodded his head toward Victoria. "She is one amazin' young lady. She gits it from her mammy. She sure was sumthin' special."

"Why isn't she with her parents?" JJ asked cautiously.

"Sad story, really." Billy stoked the fire with an iron rod. "Little Victoria's madre is a very good woman. But when de war broke out, dey put her in jail for bein' an abolitionist."

"What about her father?" Isabella shifted her position on the log. "Is he against slavery, too?"

"Her padre?" Billy shook his head. "He's a different story. He's a very evil man. Afta makin' his money running the *demon rum* off de Gulf Coast, he bought a big cotton plantation up near Cedar Key. Bought hisself a load of slaves from Africa..."

"That's horrible," answered JJ and Isabella.

Zeke shook his head disgusted. "Makes me sick to even think of it..."

"Before Victoria's ma went to jail, she helped me, Azaelia, and a couple of others escape from de plantation." Billy continued. "Den she asked if we could sneak Victoria down to Cayo Hueste...

"Key West?" JJ asked. He stood up, waving his arms over the flames.

"Yes sir." Billy nodded, tossing the iron rod in the dry sand. "Cayo Hueste. Dats what de Spanish called it when dey owned it. Victoria has an auntie down on de island. She is one amazin' little girl. She always seems to be keepin' a positive attitude."

Chapter Eighteen

The Mystery Clues

They feasted on a meal of collard greens, baked beans, and fatback. After dinner, while the others did their evening chores, Billy and the Bayway Buccaneers sat around the crackling campfire. Sparks and soot swirled upward toward the starlit sky. The warmth of the glowing embers was comforting to their still damp bodies.

"I'm sorry for what happened earlier," Billy said apologetically. "Sometimes dey can be such busybodies. We're all just scared."

"No need to apologize," Zeke said. "We're strangers, unexpected guests."

"It's not that," Billy said. "It's...."

"You don't have to explain anything to us Billy," Isabella replied. "You've been so wonderful to us already."

"Right," JJ said. "Tomorrow, after sunrise, we'll be on our way. Sure have enjoyed the hospitality...."

"Not going to be dat easy," Billy Barefoot took a long pause, a frown on his face. "Don't know what to make of your story. You is not lying ta me, I'm fer sure o' dat. But still don't understand how you got here."

"We know how you feel," Isabella gave an understanding smile. "We don't believe it either! Not really."

"Yeah," Zeke interjected. "And we're *living* it!"

"But the lighthouse," Isabella interrupted. "We've been following this map toward the lighthouse. Following the light seems to bring us closer to the future." Isabella shook her head, hearing how foolish her words *sounded.*

"Actually, we *had* been following the light," Zeke corrected. "Then the hurricane hit, so we had to change our course a little."

"Dats what I'm talking about," Billy said. "De lighthouse you been following. It was destroyed in dat stoam you was in. Back in '48, Sherrod Edwards was de light keeper den."

"The longboat?" Isabella asked.

"Yessum," Billy said. "It was Sherrod's. He an' his kin, Marvel. Dey left de Egmont island after the stoam. Never returned." Billy scratched his head, confused. "Dat was thir'teen years ago."

"Thirteen years ago?" Zeke asked. "Oh, gawd. Thirteen years!"

"But all this...You know? The time traveling." JJ pulled the gold coin out of his pocket and showed it to Billy. "It seems to have started after we found this doubloon. Has a Spanish ship on one side. It says *Yo Creo, 1528* on the other."

The campfire hissed and roared back to life. JJ placed an open hand over his eyes, shielding them from the flames shooting between the burning logs. Sparks and ashes softly swirled from the pit and into the night sky.

"The date passes us through the period of Spanish exploration," Zeke said, looking at his scribbled notes. "That we know for sure..."

"But we don't know what the words on the coin mean, if anything at all!" JJ shrugged his shoulders. "Or even if it has anything to do with us following the Egmont Lighthouse."

"Geez," Zeke reasoned. "And the lighthouse wasn't built until several hundred years after the Spanish arrived."

"You sure it was de lighthouse you been followin'?" Billy Barefoot asked. "Maybe like you says, de light on Egmont is de future, your way home. But maybe some other light's been burnin' all dees years?"

"So, the old lighthouse?" Isabella worried. "It was destroyed by the storm, just like the *Field Guide* said."

"Oh, dey built a new one 'bout three years ago." Billy shook his head, frowning. "Den some man in a fancy southern uniform by de name of Robert Lee. He came down from Vah'ginia. Said Egmont Key would be a good place for a rebel camp if de war ever came."

"Robert E. Lee?" JJ asked. "As in *General Robert E. Lee?*"

"Don't know about the general part." Billy nodded. "But, yessum, I think so. You know 'em?"

"He is.....," Isabella corrected herself. "Or rather he *will be*, one of the greatest generals in American history!"

"Yeah," Zeke added. "He's going to be the leader of the Confederate Army!"

"You kids sho do know a lot 'bout what's going ta happen in ta future," Billy said, scratching his gray beard.

"Internet," Zeke laughed. "Can find lots of stuff about history on the Internet!"

"What de Internet?" Billy was puzzled.

"Pay no attention to him, Billy," Isabella gave Zeke a firm shove. "Stop it with your 21st Century jokes."

"You won't have to worry about the Internet for quite some time!" JJ changed the subject. "So the lighthouse was rebuilt three years ago, so we're now in the year 1861?"

"Yes sir." Billy said. "Dat what I been tryin' to tell ya. The rebels have Egmont Key surrounded."

"The Civil War," Isabella shook her head sadly. "Between the North and the South..."

"Yes ma'am. Started coupla months ago. States started breakin' away from de United States when Lincoln became president. The South thinks Lincoln will abolish slavery. Sure hope so..." Billy turned his sad eyes downward. "Florida was one a de first states to go wit de South. We're all fugitives from the law now. Hopin' to get with de underground railroad to get Victoria to her auntie. Den we plans to head on to Cuba, or maybe de Bahamas!"

"The underground railroad?" Isabella repeated his words.

"Oh, yeah." JJ flipped open his field guide. "Harriet Tubman, she's the one that started the escape route. They called her Moses because she helped free slaves."

"But since de war started, the underground railroad been kinda' stopped." Billy shook his head. "But we still hopin'. Yesterday, when we met, we was looking for a boat dat might a been running with de underground railroad."

"You're welcome to take the boat." JJ offered. "I'm sure Izzy and Zeke agree that you need the boat more than we do..."

"Very kind offer. Thanks, but no. Der be too many of us." Billy smiled, toothless. Then, turning to Zeke, said. "You is in danger. Ezekiel, you is a black boy in de deep south now. De white peoples here..."

Billy stopped his train of thought. Then looking at JJ and Isabella said, "No offense, but..."

"No offense taken," Isabella dismissed the thought. "We understand..."

"...De white peoples here, dey won't know you is not a runaway." Billy Barefoot continued. "You gots to be careful Zeke..."

"Oh, yeah." Zeke looked down at his borrowed clothes. "Thanks Billy."

"About the new lighthouse, Billy," Isabella unfolded the *Letter of Marque.* "Is it working?"

"Yessum. It's workin' just like new," Billy answered. "But remember, de rebels have it now. So you gots to be real careful if you is plannin' ta go der."

"We'll be careful," JJ scanned his book for more information on the Egmont Lighthouse.

"So you think de lighthouse is your way ta home?" Billy thought a moment. "May I see de map?"

Isabella handed the now yellowed letter to Billy. JJ flashed a light beam with his pen, and Billy laughed seeing the new invention for the first time.

Recalling the adventure, Isabella traced her finger along the map from the island school, to Fort DeSoto, along Shell Key, and then eastward through North Channel.

"So here we are," Isabella pointed to Cabbage Key with her index finger. She shook her head, still disbelieving. "Somehow we're still more than 150 years from home!"

"Yeah," Zeke added. "And we still don't know how to get home!"

"And we still don't...," JJ paused, reflecting on his thoughts. "We don't know why we pass through some points in history, and not the others..."

"Still don't know what ta make of all dis," Billy grinned. "But it sho is fascinatin'!"

"Yeah," Isabella answered. "Except for JJ, we don't believe it either!"

"Whas dis'?" Billy turned to the mystery clues on the opposite side of the map.

"Oh, that?" JJ dismissed Mr. Celi's letter. "Just some silly questions our teacher gave us to answer. It's for some game we were supposed to play."

"I cain't read much," Billy apologized.

"Doesn't matter anyway," Zeke assured him. "The game's been over for quite some time."

"Whas' it say?" Billy pleaded. "Please read it. Maybe somthin' important."

"Why not?" Isabella read the directions for answering the mystery clues. "'How well do you know your local history? Let's see! The first team to get the six correct mystery answers will win a prize. Good luck....'"

"Come on, guys," JJ was frustrated. "None of these clues matter anymore. Besides, we're years away from Fort DeSoto."

"Maybe so," Zeke said. "But it won't hurt to take a look at it!"

"Please continue reading, miss," Billy said. "Let's have a look at de clues."

"'Clue 1: This prehistoric Florida mammal is not in the canine family.'"

"Wait a minute," Zeke said. "Remember back in the cave? The one we hiked through? Remember the paintings we saw?"

"Yeah. There were several species." Isabella followed his train of thought. "Which ones were not canines?"

"Mastodon." JJ attempted to seem disinterested.

"Nah. Doesn't fit in the spaces." Isabella shook her head. "Each letter needs to fit in a blank.

"What about Saber-Tooth Tiger?" JJ asked. "That fit?"

"No." Isabella grabbed a pencil from her backpack. "But Saber Tooth does!"

"Good goin'," Billy cheered. "Whas' de next one say?"

"'Clue 2: These Native Americans were the first to settle on the Pinellas peninsula.'"

"Was it the Caloosa?" Zeke asked, turning to JJ.

"No. It was the Tocobagas," JJ answered excitedly. "That fits, doesn't it?"

"Sure does!" Isabella wrote the answer down. "Tocobaga fits!"

Zeke read the third clue:

"'This Spanish explorer named Tampa Bay, 'Bay of the Cross.'"

"Panfilo De Narvaez. We saw him," Isabella exclaimed. She confidently wrote down the answer. Turning to Billy, she said, "He was a hottie!"

"Yeah, right." JJ gave Isabella a jealous laugh.

Billy gave them a puzzled look. "Read on, child!"

Go ahead Izzy," Zeke smiled. "Read the next clue. This is fun..."

"Wait a minute," JJ stopped the celebration. "Look. There's a pattern here. Every mystery clue on this checklist..." He paused. "In some way, we've lived every clue..."

"You're right," Isabella smiled broadly. "Maybe all we have to do is solve the rest of the clues..."

"Then we'll be home free!" Zeke shot to his feet, pumping his fist again. "Home free!"

"'Number 4,'" Isabella read, "He was the first to keep watch over this in 1848'". "Anything on the timeline for 1848?"

Hoo. Hoo. JJ looked up at the Barred Owl in the tree, gave it a smile, then returned to his *Field Guide*. Running his index finger along the manual's timeline, JJ answered, "Lots of stuff on *American History*. But Mr. Celi wrote clues about Florida history. Seems like mostly local stuff. Nothing on the timeline seems to fit..."

"Civil War?" Zeke asked.

"Nah. That didn't start until 1861!" Isabella dismissed the suggestion. "And there really weren't any major battles here in Florida."

"Yeah," JJ agreed. "And there has to be a local connection."

"Up in Saint Petersburg, or in Tampa?" Zeke asked Billy. "Is there a town clock? Maybe this person was in charge of keeping the official time."

"Don't rightly know," Billy thought a while. "Never heard of those names..."

"Those cities didn't exist back in 1848," JJ concluded. "Says here in the book only about five families lived in the area here..."

"Any inns around here Billy?" Isabella quizzed him. "Maybe he was an innkeeper..."

"What about the US mail," Zeke wondered. "Was he the first mail carrier in town?"

"You're such a goober," JJ held back a yawn. "They're called *postmasters.*"

"Da boat!" Billy Barefoot interrupted. "It's da boat!"

"What?" Isabella asked.

"De name o' de boat. *Sherrod Edwards,*" Billy said excitedly. "Dat name fit on de paper?"

Isabella mouthed the letters. "S-h-e-r-r-o-d E-d-w-a-r-d-s. It fits!"

"Oh, yeah," Zeke said in amazement. "You did say *Sherrod Edwards* was the first keeper of the old Egmont Lighthouse. Billy you're a genius!"

"Thanks, Billy," JJ gave him a big hand shake. "Don't think we could have solved that clue without your help!"

"Yeah, thanks," Zeke smiled broadly. "Only two more mystery clues to go..."

Letter Of Marque

The Six Mystery Clues

Directions: How well do you know your local history? Let's see! The first team to get the six correct mystery answers will win a prize. Good luck!

Clue 1: This prehistoric Florida mammal is not in the canine family.

ANSWER: Saber Tooth

Clue 2: These Native Americans were the first to settle on the Pinellas peninsula.

ANSWER: Toc obagas

Clue 3: This Spanish explorer named Tampa Bay, "Bay of the Cross."

ANSWER: Panfilo De Narvae z

Clue 4: He was the first to keep watch over this.

ANSWER: Sherro d Edwards

Clue 5: This famous Confederate officer surveyed Egmont Key prior to the start of the Civil War.

ANSWER: ___ ___ ___ ___ ___ ___   ___ ___ ___ ___

Clue 6: This future president traveled through Tampa Bay on his way to fight in the Spanish-American War.

ANSWER: ___ ___ ___ ___ ___ ___   ___ ___ ___ ___ ___ ___ ___

Chapter Nineteen

"Life Is A Journey..."

Bang! Bang! Bang! Gunfire echoed off the dark Gulf of Mexico. The brown owl, disturbed by the noise, launched from its perch and flew into the midnight darkness.

"We better put out de fire," Billy whispered. "Sounds like the rebs' are out patrolin' de bay. Dey ain't too close, but it's better to be safe..."

"What are they looking for?" JJ asked quietly.

"Don't rightly know. Mebe us," Billy answered. "We better turn in for de evening..."

"Good idea!" Isabella stood up. "I think we're all getting tired anyway. We can finish the clues in the morning when our minds are fresh!"

"Yeah, I'm exhausted." JJ sat up from his log, gave in to a big yawn. "But first, Billy, I want to give you something."

Billy watched JJ walk to the gray tent, then turned toward Isabella and Zeke. "Would ya' mind answerin' dis one question? Been on my mind since we met."

"We'll try," Zeke said.

"Well...Azaelia and Victoria," Billy hesitated, not sure how to ask the question. He wasn't sure he wanted to know the answer. "I's worried about dem. You know, wit de war going on. I's worried about dey future..."

"Billy, I really don't know how much we should tell you," Isabella said softly. Her eyes moistened. "The war will last quite a while. It'll get worse before it gets better....But the North eventually wins..."

"It does get better, really," Zeke assured him. He placed his hand on Billy Barefoot's shoulder. "Azaelia and Victoria. You won't have to worry about their future! They'll live free. They won't have to worry about being runaways all their lives."

"In the year 2004," Isabella smiled. "That's where we're from. America is a free nation where everyone has equal rights. We still have lots of work to do. But America's made lots of progress since the Civil War years."

"Just keep your faith," Zeke said. "That'll carry you through the hard times."

"Thanks," Billy smiled, his eyes glistening. "Feel better already."

JJ returned to the campsite, a T-shirt draped over his shoulder.

"Here, Billy. This is just a small token of our appreciation for all your help." JJ grabbed the sleeves, spreading open the faded shirt. "It says, *Changes in Latitudes, Changes in Attitude*. They're words from one of my favorite songs. It's not much of a gift, but the words seem to fit our situation...."

"Thank you. I believe in being kind to peoples," Billy said softly. Tears welled in his eyes as he gave JJ a hug. "And it been a pleasure meeting you."

"And you can have these beads. *Go Gators*," Zeke smiled, draping the blue and orange pirate beads around Billy's neck. "So you can remember me, too!"

"I'll never forget you! No way!" Billy gave Zeke a hug, then wiped a tear from his cheek. "You give me hope for de future."

"You're such a good man. And I won't forget all you've done for us," Isabella whispered. She reached her arms around Billy's thin body, gently kissing him on the cheek. Then, changing the subject, she said, "I hope you don't mind that we get an early start tomorrow morning. I think it's going to be another long day..."

"Not at all. We gots to get up early anyway," Billy gave a sad smile. "Every morning we walk to de bay to see if any one be there to pick us up..."

"Well good luck," JJ gave Billy a genuine smile. "It seems like we're all on some sort of journey...."

"Funny you should say dat," Billy chuckled. "Victoria's madre always be saying, *Life is a journey, make fun of it.*"

Chapter Twenty

The Egmont Passage

For a second time, the early morning silence was broken by rumbling thunder echoing off the Gulf of Mexico. Sea gulls squawked in agitation, leaving their mangrove perches in search of quieter skies. Lightning filled the sky with flashes of yellow and orange. Too exhausted from their recent adventures, the teenagers didn't wake at the first sounds of the thunder.

But it was sporadic cannon fire, playing harmony to the looming storm, that jolted them from a peaceful slumber.

"Wake up! Wake up!"

"Oh, gawd!" Zeke shot up from the gray tent, peeking through its open flap. "It happened again..."

"What happened again?" JJ yawned, his eyes struggled to open.

"Shhhh." Isabella rubbed the corners of her eyes, then gave a big yawn. "You'll wake the others."

"There are no others," Zeke responded. "They're gone! We must be in another time zone!"

The Bayway Buccaneers scanned the area with sleepy eyes. With the exception of their borrowed clothes and the tent they slept in, there was no evidence of the campsite. Billy, Azaelia, and Victoria had disappeared, along with the other families.

Cannon fire and thunder rumbled in the background while the trio quickly packed up for the day's journey. Without knowing which direction to turn, they decided to backtrack down the trail toward the *Sherrod Edwards*. Upon arrival, they let out a big sigh relief when they found the longboat undisturbed beneath the palm branches.

****

"**It's** a scattered thunderstorm. Nowhere near as threatening as the Gale of '48." Lightening reflected off the lenses of JJ's glasses. "Besides, the *Field Guide* says nothing about a hurricane hitting this area in 1861..."

"That's if we're still in 1861," Isabella stopped him mid-sentence.

"Yeah. I'm not so sure about this." Zeke's hat shifted in the wind. Grabbing it, he twisted it firmly on his head. "Shouldn't we wait for the storm to pass?"

"Nah," JJ dismissed the thought. "We'll wait for the tide to turn outward, then make our way down the bay side of Shell Key. We'll know what we're up against once we have Egmont Key in sight."

Isabella and Zeke remained hesitant but, not having a better idea, followed JJ's lead. They untied the boat, right sided it, then dragged it toward the choppy water.

"Not sure I'm ready for this again!" Isabella placed the three bags in the boat, securing them with extra nautical rope. Then sitting on the center bench, she placed an oar on her lap. "Ready."

Zeke, paddle in hand, sat on the center bench beside her. "Ready here."

JJ pointed the bow of the *Sherrod Edwards* towards the open channel. He gave the longboat a shove, then hopped back in. "Ready, row. Stroke! Stroke! Great job!"

"Wait a minute," Zeke stopped paddling. "The *Letter of Marque?*"

"Right, the mystery clues, maybe they'll tell us what's going to happen next?"

"Have it right here." Isabella reached in her pocket for the map. "Here, Zeke. You read it while we paddle."

"Come on Izzy," JJ said. "The wind's shifting on us. Gimme some help rowing! Can't you talk and row at the same time?"

"Chill out! Just stay calm. You might try to be a little kinder, too." Isabella turned her head around to Zeke. "What's the next clue say?"

"'Clue 5,'" Zeke said. "'This famous Confederate officer surveyed Egmont Key prior to the start of the Civil War.'"

"Any ideas, Izzy?" JJ asked coldly. "You're our resident military expert."

"Lots of famous Confederates," she reasoned. "But there weren't any

67

Civil War battles fought in this area."

"Didn't say anything about a battle," Zeke corrected her. "Do you know of any Confederates that were surveyors?"

"Billy Barefoot!" Isabella dug her paddle deep into the choppy water. "Maybe he said something that might give us a clue!"

The winds picked up as they moved closer to the channel and the open waters of the Gulf of Mexico. Thunder rumbled closer, drowning the sounds of cannon fire.

"I don't recall that he said anything about a surveyor." Zeke flipped the letter over to study the map, then looked up to the thundering clouds. "Sure there's not a better plan than rowing into open waters?"

"We've said all along that the lighthouse is our way home. Right?" Sweat glistened on JJ's brow. "It'd be crazy not follow it now. Especially after all we've been through."

"JJ's right," Isabella nodded. "I think getting to the Egmont Lighthouse as quickly as possible is the best plan..."

"I know," Zeke conceded. "But couldn't we wait until the storm passes?"

"Hey!" Isabella interrupted Zeke's train of thought. "Maybe the clue has something to do with the lighthouse?"

"Time to have a look around." JJ removed his glasses, wiped them clean of sea spray, then neatly stored them in his knapsack. He pulled out the binoculars.

"See anything?" Isabella asked, breathlessly.

"I think I saw a flash coming from the lighthouse!" JJ answered, focusing the binoculars.

"Sure it wasn't lightening?" Zeke asked cautiously.

"Let me have a look." Isabella took the binoculars, aiming them toward Egmont Key. "It sure is the lighthouse."

"Awesome," Zeke cheered. "Just awesome!"

"That's the best news we've had all morning." JJ rested his hand on Isabella's sholder, a big smile grew on his face.

"Look," Isabella pointed toward smoke billowing toward the dark sky. "That's where the cannon fire is coming from. I see smoke coming from old Fort Dade!"

"Lemme have a look." Zeke aimed the binoculars at the black smoke.

"Yup, it's old Fort Dade, all right!" He paused a moment. "Hey, what's that over there? Looks like something bubbling up from the bottom! It's flattening the waves. Making the choppy water flat..."

"Lemme have another look," JJ grabbed the binoculars, then focused on the flat water. "That's strange. I've only read about it...but never really saw one before..."

"I wonder if it's a school of fish," Zeke's face turned serious. "Or maybe a submarine surfacing..."

"Ooh, oh!" JJ moved the binoculars away from the flat water, focusing on the horizon. "We're in big trouble. It's that Spanish galleon that's been following us..."

"The *GhostRider?*" Isabella asked, a tremble in her voice. "The pirate ship?"

Chapter Twenty One

Tempest In A Teacup

With all the excitement, the Bayway Buccaneers failed to notice the thunderhead forming above them. Winds from the east suddenly picked up. The skies darkened, and the *Sherrod Edwards* tossed violently in the open waters. Electricity filled the air, making the hair on their necks stand on end.

Ruuuuumble! Thunder rolled above the teenagers. Then came stronger winds and a cold blanket of rain.

"Not again," Zeke shouted, above roar the of the spring thunderstorm. "I knew we should have waited out the storm."

"No time for second guessing," JJ hollered, his voice drowned out by the pounding rain. He adjusted his *Tampa Bay Buccaneer* cap to keep the driving raindrops from hitting his face. "Gotta row hard! The storm will pass..."

Flaaash! Craaaaaaaaaaaack! The first flash of lightning streaked down from a black cloud onto a mangrove island, catching it on fire.

"A burning bush." Zeke gave a nervous laugh. "Just like the Bible. Maybe God's going to pay us a visit..."

"Or someone else..." JJ worried.

"Where are we heading?" Isabella dug her oar deep into the churning water. The longboat rocked violently. "We're too far to make it to Egmont Key. Maybe we should anchor here and ride out the storm?"

"Zeke. Do you remember that flat water we noticed earlier?" JJ hollered,

70

spitting out rain water. "Think you can find it in this storm?"

"Yeah, sure," he shouted. "Why?"

JJ gave him a serious smile. "I have this idea!"

Flaaaaaaaah! Craaaaaack! Booooom! Ruuuumble. The thunderstorm raged in the black skies above them. The trio turned the longboat southward, returning to the open waters of Bunce's Pass.

Stroke, stroke!"

"Over there," Zeke shivered. "The *flat water!*"

"Good job," Isabella shouted, wiping the blonde mopping hair away from her eyes. "So JJ, I hope you have a great plan up your sleeve!"

"Not sure it will work..." JJ shook his head.. But if you're right..." Zeke pulled hard on the paddle, straining his biceps. "It's a freshwater spring shooting up from the aquifer." JJ smiled.

"A spring...?" Zeke screamed. He lifted his oar, then dug it into the dark bay water.

"Yeah. I know it sounds crazy." JJ rolled his eyes. "Izzy, I'll steer toward the flat water. When we're directly over it, I want you to toss the bow anchor out as far as you can. I'll do the same with the back anchor..."

"This is going to ruin my *Gator* cap." Zeke shook his head. Pulling off the ball cap, he dipped it into the rainwater filling the longboat. "Think your idea is going to work?"

"I hope so." Isabella tossed out the front anchor.

Splash!

"Yeah, me too." JJ heaved the back anchor. "Because I'm fresh out of ideas..."

Splash!

"It's working." Isabella smiled cautiously. "At least for now."

Chapter Twenty Two

Flat Water

The Bayway Buccaneers hunkered in the protective shell of the *Sherrod Edwards* for the second time.

"Here guys." Isabella draped her wind breaker over their heads, muffling the sounds of the thunderstorm. The rhythmic patter of the rain on the jacket was almost soothing.

"The flat water won't give us any protection from the lightning," JJ explained. "But I read about this phenomenon in some old Florida newspaper..."

"You're making this up," Zeke teased. "Aren't you?"

"No, really," JJ insisted. "The news story said that fishermen used to anchor off in the flat waters of these kinds of Gulf springs during storms. Seems that the mixture of warm and cold water had some sort of calming effect on the water's surface..."

"Doesn't matter if you are making it up," Isabella chuckled. "It seems to be working, and *that's* what matters..."

"You guys," JJ said incredulously. "I can't believe you guys are *dissing* me!"

"Not to change the subject, or anything," Isabella smiled, changing the subject. "Mind if we check the field guide? Maybe there's something in there to help us solve the next clue?"

"Yeah," Zeke said sarcastically. "Any hurricanes we need to know about?"

"Let's get serious." Isabella admonished him.

"Okay, okay!" Zeke turned serious. "The clue says something about a famous Confederate who surveyed Egmont Key before the war!" Zeke counted the answer spaces on the mystery clue. "There are six spaces for the first name. One space for the middle initial. And three for the last name..."

"It's gotta be General Lee!" Isabella shouted. "Billy Barefoot said *Robert E. Lee* checked out Egmont."

JJ flipped through the *Florida Field Guide*, looking for references to General Robert E. Lee. "Not too much stuff on Lee..."

"Did General Lee ever even travel this far south...?" Zeke reread the clue.

"Wait a minute..." JJ shouted, careful to keep raindrops from hitting the pages of his book. "Says here that *Colonel* Robert E. Lee, surveyed Egmont Key before the war to see if the Confederate Army could use it..."

"*If the Civil War ever came...*" Isabella completed JJ's sentence. "Just like Billy said!"

"And the letters fit..." Zeke shouted. "You da bomb, Izzy. You solved mystery clue number five!"

With a final flash of lightning, the thunderstorm safely moved out to sea.

Chapter Twenty Three

Pirates!

"Oh, no!" Zeke peeked from underneath Isabella's jacket. "Can't see a darn thing. The storm blew in a blanket of fog!"

"Now what?" Isabella waved her hand in the milky air. "Hey, is that the lighthouse?"

Zeke craned his neck around. "Looks like it...Think we should row in that direction..."

"I say we stay anchored awhile to see what the fog does." JJ looked up, then opened to the *Pirates of the Caribbean* chapter in his book. "I think it's safer where we're at right now..."

"I guess you're right." Isabella agreed. "Let's try to solve the last mystery clue..."

"Not worried about that either." JJ shook his head. "That pirate ship. We rowed in the direction of that pirate ship..."

"Oh, gawd," Zeke worried. "I tried to forget about it."

"Look at this picture." JJ shoved the book in front of them. "It's a Spanish galleon. Just like the *GhostRider*..."

"Read what it says, JJ," Isabella said eagerly.

"*The Tradewinds of the early 1500's brought a reign of terror across the Atlantic Ocean to the Caribbean Sea, and Gulf of Mexico."* JJ adjusted the reading glasses on the bridge of his nose. "*Pirates followed the explorers and colonists to the New World. Pirates like Blackbeard, Black Bart, and Gasparilla, took to the seas in search of ships carrying silver, gold, and other treasures. They were mostly criminals, and good-sailors-gone-bad..."'*

"See, I told you they were good-for-nothing people," Zeke interrupted.

JJ continued reading the passage in the book. *"'...some were fugitive slaves working to earn their freedom. Still, some were simply caught by the lure of adventures on the seas. All were in it for the plundering and pilfering...'"*

Bang! Sea gull feathers floated in the evening breeze

"What's that?" JJ asked, looking up from his book. "Sounds like gunfire."

"Can't be sure of it..." Isabella wiped the mist from her face. "The fog's muffling the sound..."

Clink-clack. Clink-clack. Clink-clack.

"I hear something else, too!" Zeke interrupted. "It sounds like metal rubbing on something!"

"Yeah," Isabella said. "Maybe it's gunfire from Old Fort Dade?"

"Can't see a darn thing," JJ waived his hand in the misty air. White feathers swirled, then fell to the floor of the longboat.

"I don't like this," Zeke hollered.

"Me neither." JJ stuffed the book in his knapsack. "We better pack up and get ready for a quick swim. Gimmee the *Letter of Marque*, and anything else you want to keep dry..."

"Good idea." Zeke handed over the notepad and pen. "Don't want to lose my notes. It's going to be one heck of a story...."

Bang! More feathers rained down on the tiny longboat.

"Don't know what it is." Isabella whispered, waving her hand. "And what's with these feathers?"

Clink-clack. Clink-clack. Clink-clack. Splash!

Chapter Twenty Four

GhostRider

It was late 19th Century Florida, and the Civil War had long been over. Years earlier, America's Northern army defeated the South, freeing America's slaves forever. The United States, including Florida, was rebuilding from a war that had forced Billy Barefoot and his family to be on the run. The Bayway Buccaneers, although their memories were still warmed by Billy's kindness, turned their attention to solving the sixth mystery clue. The trio was in the midst of discussion when they were stopped cold by the sound of gun fire and raining sea gull feathers coming from the morning fog.

By 1872, America's strong naval fleet had put an end to the golden age of piracy. But that didn't matter to the men haunting the *GhostRider*. They were given orders to search and retrieve three runaway teenagers.

The sailor in the crow's nest kept a watchful eye for invading ships. Was he watching for *English* ships, or *Spanish* ships, today? Between the native Indians, Spaniards, the English, and the Americans, *La Florida* had changed hands more often than a pieces of eight. In the more than 500 years he had been in the crow's nest, it was impossible for him to remember who owned the Florida peninsula.

"I hate General Zaragoza...." Jean-Denis fired his pistol at the flying sea gull.

Bang! Gull feathers burst in the air like white fireworks.

"Any sign of them?" The French pirate shouted up to the sailor in the crow's nest. Jean-Denis blew smoke from the barrel of the flintlock pistol, then rested it on the bow rail of the *GhostRider*.

"Still 'ave a clear view of the horizon," the sailor shouted down, a spyglass pressed against his right eye. "But 'aven't seen them since the fog..."

"Oui," the French pirate agreed. "It does look like we're sailing on a cloud."

"Shall I keep on looking?" The sailor scratched the stubble on his chin with the spyglass.

"Oui." The pirate nodded his head, then replied in a thick French accent, "Keep searching while we prepare to anchor. Captain Lopez has given the order to drop the sails and raise the *Jolie Rouge*. He says the time has come to bring them aboard. We'll send out the longboats to find them...if we have to..."

"Aye, aye, Jean-Denis." The pirate gave him a salute with his razor-sharp cutlass. "Aye, aye."

The fat metal chains rubbed against the hull of the Spanish galleon as they followed the anchors down into Tampa Bay.

Clink-clack. Clink-clack. Clink-clack. Splash! The bow anchor fell cleanly, splashing into the misty waters.

Clink-clack. Clink-clack. Clink-clack. Crash! The starboard anchor came down hard, shattering the bow of the *Sherrod Edwards*.

Chapter Twenty Five

Cold Harbor

Craaack! Crunch! Splash!

Splinters flew in every direction. The bow shattered, planks of wood drifted into the open waters of the Gulf of Mexico. What remained of the longboat shuddered violently in the mist, plunging the teenagers into the cold water. Then, making one final gurgle, the stern of the *Sherrod Edwards* flipped upside down, bobbing in the chilly bay.

"Oh, gawd!" Zeke choked back a mouthful of saltwater. "What the...?"

"You okay?" Isabella gasped, grabbing onto to the derelict longboat. "I lost my backpack..."

Bang! Gull feathers continued to rain down in the moist air.

"Yeah, fine," Zeke coughed, sucking in sea water with air.

"Here, take my hand," Isabella reached out to Zeke. "Where's JJ?"

"JJ!" Zeke called out. "Where are you?"

"JJ," Isabella's voice quivered in the cold water. "Can you hear me?..."

"I'm fine." JJ swam toward their voices. "Here, Izzy. Grab onto the satchel and knapsack...I'll be right back..."

"Where you..."

JJ swam back into the blanket of fog.

"Where do you think he's going?" Isabella worried.

"I dunno..." Zeke answered.

Waiting for his return, Isabella and Zeke held on helplessly to the remains of the *Sherrod Edwards*. Debris from the broken boat drifted past

78

the Egmont Lighthouse flashing in the misty distance.

"Oh, gawd, it's freezing out here." Zeke strained his eyes on the flashing beacon. "Think it's too far to swim?"

"I don't know..." Isabella shivered. Tears streamed down her face. "I'm so worried about JJ. Where did he go?..."

"Over here!" JJ hollered. "I'm fine!"

"Thank God you're okay," Isabella sobbed. "You had me so worried. Where did you go?..."

"Had to rescue this..." JJ flopped the soggy Teddy Bear on the hull of the shattered longboat. "Knew how important he was to you. But couldn't save your book bag..."

"Oh, JJ..." Isabella cried. "That was so romantic..."

"...It started drifting out on the Gulf stream." JJ laughed through watery eyes. "Eventually it would have made it to Cuba. Couldn't stand the thought of Castro having it..."

"Hey guys. Sorry to interrupt your Kodak moment." Zeke pointed to barnacles clinging to the giant wooden hull. "But what's that...?"

"It's a shh shh shh ship..." JJ stammered. "Looks like the pirate ship."

A rope ladder unfurled from above, splashing in the water near the bobbing teenagers.

"Good day." The pirate called down to the teenagers. "Welcome aboard."

Chapter Twenty Six

The French Pirate Redux

Much of Nasty Juan's crew on the *GhostRider* lay sprawled on the main deck near kegs of rum. The pirate on guard duty, an ex-convict from Hispaniola, lay drunk against the main mast, his index finger wrapped around the trigger of a pistol.

The Bayway Buccaneers were escorted to Jean-Denis at knife point. They stood before the pirate dripping wet.

The French pirate carefully aimed his *Bourgeoys* flintlock.

"Sacre Blue," Jean-Denis said. "This one's for Napoleon III..."

Bang! White feathers filled the air, falling onto the deck of the Spanish galleon. White feathers stuck to the still-soggy teenagers.

Jean-Denis turned toward the captive trio, then angrily eyed the armed pirates. "Put the knives down, you drunken fools. These kids are the guests of Captain Lopez."

The French pirate dismissed the guards, then offered his apologies for the manner in which they were welcomed aboard the Spanish galleon.

"Please allow me to reintroduce myself." The pirate bowed in a grand gesture. "I am the First Officer, Jean-Denis Godet, from Corsica. Most famous for my pirate skills on the Barbary Coast....and of course, the Caribbean Sea..."

"I'm Isabella. Pleased to meet you again." She stepped forward, plucking a feather pasted to her dripping forehead. "You gave me these beads at Pavilion 29."

"Oui. And the turquoise still looks quite lovely on you." The French pirate gave a serious smile. "We've been following you for quite some time. Been waiting to get you aboard the *GhostRider*..."

"...And remember me, Ezekiel?" Zeke stammered. "Please call me Zeke."

"But of course." Jean-Denis smiled, shaking his hand. "How's the story going?"

"It's not the story that I planned to write..." Zeke smiled back, "...but it should be pretty interesting..."

"And I'm..." JJ reached out an open hand.

"Oui. I know who you are, JJ Lopez. The Captain is expecting you. But first we need to get you cleaned up." Jean-Denis placed the pistol in his belt, then turned his eyes toward the teenagers. "Where on the high seas did you get those clothes?"

"From Billy Barefoot." JJ shifted the knapsack on his shoulders. "Met him back on Cabbage Key..."

"Oui. Quite a noble gentleman." The pirate nodded.

"You know him?..." Isabella asked, squeezing water from her soggy bear.

"But of course. Azaelia, and Victoria, too!" Jean-Denis nodded again, then stared at their ragged clothes. Changing the subject he said, "We can't have you meeting Nasty Juan looking like that. You look like runaways..."

"Nasty Juan?" Zeke gasped.

"My apologies. Those who have been terrorized by Captain Lopez know him by that name. But his friends call him Juan Jon Lopez." Jean-Denis flicked a feather off Zeke's shoulder. "Again, please accept my apologies for the manner in which you came aboard. We truly did not intend to drop anchor on you...The crew on this ship..."

The trio stared at the drunken pirates on the decks of the *GhostRider*. The sailor on guard duty, his finger still on the pistol trigger, reached his empty hand toward a pewter tankard. He took a long drink of rum, winced, then returned to a peaceful slumber.

"...just can't get good help anymore," Jean-Denis shook his head, disgusted. "All they want to do is rock the boat all night..."

"...and party everyday..." Zeke gave a nervous laugh. "Yeah! I know the song..."

JJ and Isabella laughed in nervous unison.

Chapter Twenty Seven

Hardtack

Jean-Denis Godet ordered the cabin boy to fetch a change of clothes for the guests of Captain Juan Jon Lopez. He then escorted the teenagers below deck to the ship's galley.

"Help yourself to lunch," Jean-Denis said. "Plenty of rice and beans aboard this ship. Turkey jerky and hardtack, too."

"Hardtack?"

"Oui," Jean-Denis nodded. "Dry biscuits. They are quite common around here."

"Gee, thanks, Mr. Godet," they answered.

"Please, call me Jean-Denis. We are almost like family." He smiled. "What would you like to drink? There's tea in the pot."

"How about some root beer?" Zeke grinned. "With a scoop of vanilla ice cream on top!"

"You're under age!" Jean-Denis replied. "Let's just stick with the tea..."

"Just ignore him, Jean-Denis," Isabella gave Zeke a nasty look. "It's another one of his jokes..."

"Oui." The French pirate gave a serious look. "American humor."

Jean-Denis walked toward the galley door. Then turned toward JJ. "I'll be back in a while for your introduction to the Captain. He will be delighted to finally meet you. In the meantime, make yourselves comfortable."

Jean-Denis Godet closed the door behind him.

****

"**What** was Jean-Denis talking about?" Isabella said, flicking another gull feather off her shoulder. She turned to JJ. "Have you ever heard of Juan Jon Lopez?"

"I've read about lots of pirates," JJ shook his head, "but I never heard of *Nasty Juan*, or Juan Jon Lopez!"

"Yeah, JJ." Zeke unbuttoned Billy Barefoot's borrowed shirt. "This is sure some strange coincidence. Jean-Denis said he knew Billy and Azaelia..."

"Victoria, too," Isabella interjected. "He also said something about Captain Lopez expecting you. As if he knows who you are..."

"I don't know what he's talking about!" JJ dumped the wet contents of the knapsack onto the galley table. The gold doubloon clanked down, spun a few times, then wobbled to a halt. JJ picked up his book, then pawed through its soggy pages. "I never knew my parents, and I don't know anything about my family..."

"Your initials, *JJ*." Isabella grabbed the clothes Jean-Denis gave her. She moved across the galley floor toward a pantry. "What do the letters mean?"

"Someone once told me it stood for Juan Jackson." JJ replied defensively. "Was told I was named after Andrew Jackson, the first governor of Florida."

"So your full name is *Juan Jackson Lopez?*" Isabella asked.

"I don't really know, Izzy," JJ shot back. "I've always just been called *JJ Lopez*."

"Don't be so defensive." Zeke defended Isabella. "She's just trying to figure this out!"

"Yeah," Isabella nodded. "Don't take counsel of your fears..."

"What?" JJ gave her an angry look. "*Don't take counsel of my fears!* What the heck's that supposed to mean?"

"What I'm trying to get at..." Isabella took a long pause. "I think the three of us have already figured out that Captain Lopez is somehow related to you..."

"Are you loco?" JJ shook his head. "How do you figure that?"

"...And I think you're afraid to learn anything about your past." Isabella insisted. "You're afraid of what you might find..."

"That's crazy, Izzy." JJ waved her off.

"What about *Juan?*" Zeke admired his new buccaneer outfit from the reflection of a cutlass he found in the corner. He waved the sword back

83

and forth, slicing the air into tiny pieces. "Do you think it's a family name?"

"Don't have a clue. I grew up in foster homes, remember? Never even seen my birth certificate. As I said, JJ is the only name people have called me..." JJ paused, annoyed at the interrogation by his friends. "But in case you don't remember, before we came aboard this ship, we were worried about getting into a crossfire between the Rebels and Yankees..."

"...What's your point anyway?" Isabella ducked behind a pantry closet. "Don't come in here boys...I'm changing into dry clothes."

"My point is..." JJ replied in a deliberate, slow voice. "The GhostRider is an old Spanish galleon. Probably stolen from the king's naval fleet..."

"How can you be sure?" Zeke returned the cutlass to the corner. His eyes turned to JJ.

"I just know. I've studied this stuff enough." JJ leafed through the moist pages of the field guide. "Remember this picture of the ship?"

"Sure," Zeke nodded. "That's the one you showed us before the anchor crashed on us..."

"Well the book says it was built in 1528!" JJ said seriously. "And..."

"Da, dah!" Isabella came out twirling, wearing a turban-like hat, and loose fitting overcoat and pants. "Well, how do I look?"

"You look like Mary Read. She was one brave pirate." JJ's frown changed to a proud smile. "Just like you, Izzy..."

"Gee, thanks." She moved closer to JJ, her black-buckled shoes clanking on the wooden floor. "It was built in 1528? So what are you saying? That we time-traveled backwards, and now we're on one of Narvaez's ships?"

"I don't think we've time-traveled. But it may be worse," JJ answered, his face grew more serious. "I think we're on a pirate ghost ship!"

"A ghost ship?" Zeke answered. "Oh, gawd!"

"Are you kidding?" Isabella shot JJ a strange look. "Why would you say such a thing?"

"That's the only explanation!" JJ nodded. "We first met Jean-Denis back at Pavilion 29. That was in 2004. Right?"

"Yes, but that doesn't..." Isabella responded.

"Listen, Izzy. The ship is called the GhostRider, and it was built in the 1500's. And now we meet Jean-Denis again in the 1800's." JJ explained. "What other answer could there be?"

"What about the last mystery clue?" Zeke said, remembering the Letter of Marque. "Maybe it can give us another explanation..."

The trio, now fully dressed in pirate attire, clustered around the Letter of Marque. They spread it out on the dining table as Isabella doled out pieces of hardtack.

"This stuff's awful." Zeke swallowed the dry biscuit, then chased it with a gulp of black tea.

"Let's try some of that turkey-jerkey." JJ gave a sour look, crunching on the final bite of the hardtack.

"Here." Isabella tore off a piece of dry meat. "It's a little salty, but it's good."

"Read the last clue, Zeke," JJ pointed to the wet map. He chewed hard on the dry meat. "Maybe you're right. Maybe there is another explanation..."

Zeke dragged his finger down to the last line on the letter, reading the sixth clue:

"'This future president traveled through Tampa Bay on his way to fight in the Spanish-American War.'"

"Excuse moi." The galley door creaked open. "I could not help but hear your conversation. You are right to follow the mystery clue...But the final clue will be solved much later..."

Zeke and JJ shot up from their seat, trying to hide the Letter of Marque. Isabella, startled at Jean-Denis' sudden arrival, sat with her mouth wide open.

"It's okay, we already know about the Letter of Marque." The French pirate stepped forward.

"You do?" Isabella struggled to regain her composure.

"Oui. And the gold doubloon, too!" Jean-Denis placed a firm hand on JJ's shoulder. "Captain Lopez is ready to meet you." He turned to Isabella and Zeke. "Of course, you are invited, too!"

Chapter Twenty Eight

"Juan Jon Lopez"

Jean-Denis Godet led the trio through the maze of doors and gangways in the hollows of the Spanish galleon. The *GhostRider* shifted side-to-side on the calm afternoon waters. Light from the French pirate's oil lantern cast sinister shadows on the dank walls.

Knock, knock, knock. "Good afternoon, my captain," Jean-Denis said respectfully. "Your guests are here."

"Come in my friends. Your new outfits look quite nice on you!" Captain Juan Jon Lopez said in a low, breathless voice. He made eye contact with JJ. "I have waited for your arrival for quite some time."

The teenagers entered the stateroom, lit only by two candles and Jean-Denis' lantern. Nasty Juan sat up in a large, wood-framed bed, his body covered to the chest by an ornate cover.

"Please have a seat." He pointed to the wooden bench near his bedside. He gave a weak smile. "I understand your arrival was...shall we say...a bit extraordinary..."

The Bayway Buccaneers laughed nervously.

"I do apologize for the incompetency of my crew." The captain's voice was weak and labored.

"Captain Lopez, with all due respect..." JJ paused to find the right words. "We're quite confused as to our being here..."

"Patience, my son," Captain Lopez reached for JJ's hand. "It is a virtue that you must learn."

"Will that be all, Captain?" Jean-Denis asked.

"Please ask the cabin boy to send some hot tea." Captain Lopez adjusted the bedcover. "Thank you."

"Oui." Jean-Denis took his leave in search of the cabin boy.

Juan Lopez turned to his guests. "I'm sure it is all confusing."

"Good afternoon, sir," Isabella hesitated, not sure if she should speak. "I'm Isabella, and this is Zeke. Jean-Denis mentioned that you know about our *Letter of Marquis*..."

"...And the doubloon," Zeke finished her sentence. "You know about the gold coin, too?"

"Oh, yes! I know about the mystery clues and the map." Captain Lopez gave a weak chuckle. "I don't mean to make light of your questions. But I know all about your journey!"

The pirate captain paused, allowing his guests to process the new information. "Please allow me to start with an introduction. My name is Juan Jon Lopez, captain of the Spanish galleon, *GhostRider*...."

"Please, Captain Lopez," JJ pleaded. "What does this all have to do with us?"

"It's all about you!" Captain Lopez tapped JJ on the chest. "This has nothing to do with your friends here..."

"I don't understand, sir." Isabella shook her head. "Then why are Zeke and I here?"

"It wasn't planned that way." The pirate captain coughed. "When JJ found the coin...Well, we had no idea he would take you with him on this journey. The three of you must be special friends..."

"What do you mean?" Zeke asked cautiously.

Captain Juan Lopez took a deep, raspy breath. "Let me start from the beginning...

"I am Captain Juan Jon Lopez, from Barcelona, Spain. I was a commissioned officer in the navy of King Charles I. That was back in 1528, when I was sent to the Spanish Main on an expedition led by Panfilo de Narvaez..."

"You sailed with Narvaez?" JJ's eyes widened.

"Sí. Our mission was to explore *La Florida* for its many riches. We were to bring back gold and silver for the Spanish crown. I did not believe in the mission, nor the slavery that would allow it to happen..."

"Why did you go?" Zeke adjusted his position on the wooden bench.

"It was my duty." Captain Lopez nodded seriously. "Before crossing the Atlantic we headed into the Mediterranean Sea. Along the coast of

France..."

"Is that where you met Jean-Denis Godet?" Isabella leaned forward.

"Si. His reputation for fighting the corsairs on the Barabary Coast was well known." Captain Lopez plucked a stray gull feather from her hair. "Jean-Denis is a bit peculiar. But he is a fine First Officer..."

"Why does he hate seagulls?" JJ stared at the feather in Nasty Juan's fingers.

"It's not the gulls at all." Captain Lopez chuckled. "Today is Cinco de Mayo..."

"Mexican Independence Day?" JJ gave him a confused look. "Today is May 5th?"

"Si." Juan Jon Lopez laughed. "Today is the anniversary of the Battle of Puebla, when the outnumbered Mexican army defeated the French army. Jean-Denis Godet goes on a shooting spree every year at this time...."

"So he takes out his anger on the seagulls?" Isabella shook her head. "How weird..."

"No. Last year it was brown pelicans." Captain Lopez shook his head. "I did say he was peculiar..."

Knock. Knock. Knock. The cabin boy entered the Captain's quarters to serve hot black tea and jerky. "Sir, your tea."

"Have some tea and turtle jerky." Captain Lopez passed the silver tray around. "Now where was I?

"...Upon our arrival in Bahia de la Cruz...what you now call Tampa Bay...we were given orders to destroy the Tocobaga villages. The Indians were slaughtered at the hands of my men!" He shook his head. "Women, children. It didn't matter, we were doing the king's work..."

"...That's horrible." Isabella covered her mouth with her hand. "How could you do such a thing?"

Captain Lopez ignored Isabella's stinging words. "When Narvaez left to explore the interior of La Florida, he ordered me and another officer to remain behind. We were given command of two Spanish galleons...."

"What happened to the other ship?" JJ asked.

"The Narvaez expedition traveled by land, up to what is now St. Marks. The other ship was wrecked in a summer squall." Juan Jon Lopez turned to Isabella, his eyes moist. "It was indeed horrible. After the senseless murder of innocent people, I and my two sons, along with the rest of the crew, voted to mutiny. We renamed the ship, GhostRider..."

"...That's when you became a pirate?" JJ asked the pirate captain.

"More or less." Captain Lopez gave a slight nod. "After many years of *pirating along the Gulf Coast, I became known as the* Nasty Juan...*Way before the other pirates came along like Black Bart and Gasparilla...."*

"...How come there's nothing about you in the history books?" Zeke asked pointedly.

"Bad public relations, *I guess."* Captain Lopez shrugged his shoulders. Then, shaking his head added, *"Can't believe you honor Gasparilla with an entire week of festivities..."*

"We were hoping to sit with the mayor at this year's Gasparilla parade," JJ grinned. *"But being with you is much more exciting..."*

"Thanks, JJ." Captain Lopez smiled with appreciation. *"Now where was I...After we mutinied, the crew set up a stronghold over on Egmont Key. There wasn't much to plunder at first. But when the word got out about the* New World...*Well, the explorers came to the Americas in droves...*

"...What happened then?" JJ hung on every word.

"We plundered and pilfered any ship sailing under the Spanish flag. We buried our treasures on Libero Cay...*that's what we called Egmont Key at the time. We set up a small pirate camp back in the sand pines. Even minted our own doubloons, so we could trade with the English and French who eventually sailed the Gulf Coast..."*

"Is that where this coin came from?" JJ retrieved the doubloon from his pirate britches. *"I found this in the artesian well..."*

"Sí!" He smiled. *"I'm familiar with it."*

"What's Yo Creo?*"* JJ asked, thumbing the coin.

"Well, that is a part of your journey you must learn for yourself." Captain Lopez smiled, then continued. *"No government ship was safe when the* GhostRider *was around..."*

"But it sounds like you were fighting for a good cause," Isabella interrupted. She set her tea cup on the floor. *"You were fighting a war against legalized corruption."*

"Yeah." JJ smiled. *"Like a* Robin Hood of the High Seas!*"*

"Sí." Captain Lopez agreed. He took a sip of his tea.

"Someone had to stop the greed of the explorations," Zeke added. *"And the slavery..."*

"Exploring new lands for the sake of knowledge and understanding...Well, that's one thing," JJ continued. *"But conquering the land. Trying to change the lives of the native peoples...That's just wrong..."*

"Sí, sí.. You shipmates have a kind heart. It will serve you well in life." Captain Lopez smiled. *"For a while we, too, were doing the work of the*

people. But we lost our vision. Became less demanding of ourselves, and what we believed in. We allowed greed to blind us..."

"How so?" Isabella asked.

"We had become intoxicated by the desire for treasure, even though we no longer had a need for it." Captain Lopez shook his head. "We became the very people we hated the most...maybe even worse than the king's men."

"Why couldn't you get out of the pirate trade?" Zeke asked, adjusting the red sash on his waist.

"Eventually, I did get out of the business." Captain Lopez wiped his eyes. "Unfortunately, the damage I had caused was far reaching. By then, my sons had already moved on to form their own pirate confederacies. One moved down to Cayo Hueste, another to the Caribbean..."

He turned his moist pirate eyes downward, then up again, pinching JJ gently on the cheek. "As for you Juan Jon Lopez, you're probably wondering what the devil all this has to do with you..."

"...Juan Jon Lopez?" JJ gasped. "That's my name?"

"Yes." The pirate captain reached over to JJ, giving him a firm hug. "We are family," he whispered.

"I knew it," Isabella whispered, wiping a tear from her cheek.

"Family?" Zeke repeated the words.

"Never hugged family before..." JJ sniffled, his voice quivering. "How are we family?"

Knock, knock, knock.

"Excuse moi, Captain." Jean-Denis Godet entered the room. "It is time for your afternoon walk on the deck."

Chapter Twenty Nine

The Voodoo Pirate's Curse

Captain Lopez and the teens walked the decks of the Spanish Galleon. The thunderstorm and fog earlier in the day had moved out to sea, leaving behind a clear, sunny afternoon. The sun burned brightly as the pirates busily untangled knots, and scraped the barnacles off the sides of the pirate ship. Any sign of the pirate party earlier in the day had been washed away by the buckets and mops of the sailors swabbing the decks.

"This one's for Napoleon III," Jean-Denis said angrily, raising his flintlock pistol in the air.

Bang! White feathers flew across the bow as another sea gull met its demise.

"Good afternoon, Jean-Denis." Captain Lopez smiled. "I see you are still celebrating Cinco de Mayo..."

"Oui, Captain." Jean-Denis greeted the pirate captain with a salute. "How is your visit coming along?"

"Quite revealing." JJ smiled.

"I was just about to tell my young buccaneers about the Voodoo Pirate." Juan Jon Lopez led the trio along the railing of the ship.

"The Voodoo Pirate?" Zeke quickly pulled out his pen and notepad from his pirate pants and began to write.

"When I was ready to give up being Nasty Juan..." Captain Lopez continued, "the crew agreed to sail the *GhostRider* back to Spain where I was to live an anonymous life as Juan Jon Lopez. But before reaching the coast of what is now Haiti, we were ambushed by an *Arawak* pirate named Quisqueya. He was known throughout the Caribbean as the Voodoo Pirate..."

"Voodoo?" Isabella repeated. A westerly breeze caressed Isabella's long blonde hair, making her curls dance on her shoulders. "As in *black magic?*"

"Si. We all had heard of Quisqueya." Captain Lopez nodded his head. "Even up here in the Gulf of Mexico. But nobody believed he was anything but crazy from drinking too much rum..."

"We noticed that rum's been a bit of a problem on this ship, too!" Zeke laughed.

"Si," the pirate captain agreed. "As you might imagine, Quisqueya and his men were not welcomed aboard our ship. We nearly killed half of his crewe before he got the advantage on the crewe of the *GhostRider*. The skirmish ended when Quisqueya ran me through with his sword...right here." He pointed to his belly.

"He ran you through?" Isabella turned her head.

"Si. With a huge cutlass" The pirate captain laughed. "It's okay, Isabella, that was a long time ago. It doesn't hurt anymore."

"How awful." Isabella closed her eyes.

"But as I lay bleeding on the quarterdeck of the *GhostRider*," Juan Jon Lopez cast his eyes downward, sighing. "Quisqueya said these final words:

Curses onto you and this ship. You will find no peace and rest until such time as your heirs make good of their futures."

"He cursed you? Zeke wrote the word *curse* in his notepad, then underlined it. "So you've been sailing this Spanish galleon all these years...?"

"Si. Nobody seems to live, or die, aboard the *GhostRider*. We've all been *spirits* since the curse of the Voodoo Pirate." Captain Lopez dabbed a tear from the corner of his eye, then turned to Isabella and Zeke. "Now if you will excuse us, young Juan Jon and I must have a private talk. I'm sure JJ will fill you in on any details you might need to know."

Chapter Thirty

Pirate Looks At 14

It was late evening on the calm gulf waters when Captain Lopez and JJ took their private walk on the decks of the *GhostRider*. The full moon slowly rose over the eastern horizon, flooding the deck with soft light. The moonbeam, a blue hue, reflected on the glassy water near Egmont Key. The ship, still at anchor with its lines pulled tight, creaked to the rhythm of the waves.

Juan Jon Lopez motioned JJ up the quarterdeck. Frail and thin, Captain Lopez leaned on the bow rail to hold his balance. The bright moonlight shone kindly on the weathered face of the once-feared *Nasty Juan*. He pointed to the dark red stain on the floor of the quarterdeck. "This is where it happened."

"Quisqueya's curse?" JJ stared at the blood stain on the deck.

"Si. The curse!" Captain Lopez nodded. "*Curses onto you and this ship. You will find no peace and rest until such time as your heirs make good of their futures!*"

JJ stepped over the sleeping night watchmen, then stepped up to the quarterdeck. "What did he mean by that?"

"Most men on this ship, they seem to have accepted their destiny. They work the sails by day, then party by night! Their lives seem to serve no sense of real purpose at all..."

"...But isn't *acceptance* a virtue?" JJ asked, his loose shirt ruffling in the breeze.

"Si." Captain Lopez smiled with conviction. "But knowing that you can change your destiny..." He pointed a finger upward. "...Ahh! That is true wisdom!"

"I don't get it." JJ shook his head.

"It is ironic, and there's no pun intended here..." the pirate captain laughed. "...But Quisqueya's voodoo has actually been a doubled-edged sword. Both a curse *and* a blessing..."

"A blessing?" JJ asked.

"Don't you see? You are my *heir*," the pirate captain clarified. "Because of the curse, I am with you with the hope of *making good on your future*..."

"*Making good on my future?*" JJ asked, staring into Juan Jon Lopez' eyes..

"Si. We have a second chance to make things right for you, and the generations to follow." Captain Lopez leaned against a rum barrel. "Please have a seat. What I have to tell you will be difficult to..."

"I don't get it." JJ took his seat on a wooden crate. "You're scaring me..."

"I don't know how much I should tell you, or even *if* I should..." Captain Lopez squeezed his eyes shut, trying to conjure the exact words. "When a man dies, he leaves behind a legacy..."

"A legacy?" JJ asked.

"Si. Sort of like a family's heritage." Captain Lopez gazed toward the flashing light on Egmont Key. "The one I have left behind was one of terror. My sons raised their children to be pirates. My irresponsible actions set off a chain reaction that has lasted for centuries. Pirates in the Caribbean. Rumrunners in the Florida Keys. We are a family of thieves..."

"Rumrunners?" JJ repeated the word, disbelieving it. "And thieves?"

The *GhostRider* rocked slowly back and forth, creaking on the soft waves.

"Your parents...," Captain Lopez dabbed his eyes. "...were smugglers down in the 10,000 islands..."

"They were what?" JJ gave him a shocked look. "My parents were smugglers?"

"Si. I'm sure they love you very much. But the lives they chose to lead..." Captain Lopez shook his head. "As an infant you lived down in Everglades City. That was before the county government took you away from your parents..."

"But why?" JJ put his hands in his face. "Why did they take me away?"

"Your parents and some other smugglers went out on airboats to rendezvous with some Colombian dealers. But it was a setup by the police.

The others were arrested, but your parents got away..." Captain Lopez wiped his face with the back of his hand. "No one knows for sure where they are right now. But that is why your past has been hidden from you...until now."

"But why...?" JJ sobbed, his voice muffled through his hands. "Why haven't they come to see me?"

"In their own way they have." Captain Lopez gently squeezed his shoulder. "Your parents are the ones who made the arrangements for you to attend the boarding school..."

"The Bayway Island Boarding School?" JJ looked up, taking a deep breath. "You know about the school?"

"Si," Captain Lopez nodded. "But no one is to know of their involvement. It is too dangerous."

"But can I meet them?" JJ asked.

"No. Like the rest of us, they already chose their path of crime. Now they are on the run..." Captain Lopez shook his head. "But you, it's not too late to change your course..."

"What do you mean?" JJ wiped his tears with a shirt sleeve.

"I am well aware of the choices you've already made in your young life." Captain Lopez nodded his head. "And I know why you made them..."

"You know about the stolen tests?" JJ gave him a startled look.

"Si," Captain Lopez said softly. "I know you are an angry young man. Remember, you have no say in the past, but you do have a say in your future."

"But," JJ sniffled, "it's not that easy..."

"Si. It won't be easy," the pirate captain interrupted. "But do not allow others...or even circumstances...make the choices that are yours to make. You are 14 with your life's journey ahead. You must believe in yourself. You must chart the course that is rightly yours..."

Chapter Thirty One

"...Right On Schedule"

Zeke and Isabella joined Captain Lopez and young Juan Jon Lopez on the quarterdeck of the Spanish galleon. Along the way, they passed a cleanup crew preparing for another midnight *pirate party*. A handful of men, some hanging from sail lines, others sprawled out in the salty air, lay lifeless as the ship remained at anchor.

"Watch your step, shipmates," the captain warned, as Isabella and Zeke walked up the steps of the quarterdeck. "Sometimes they're more dangerous in this condition, than they are awake."

The evening air cooled to a comfortable temperature. The *Jolie Rouge* flew high on the main mast, flapping in the gentle wind.

"So this happens *every* night?" Isabella asked in amazement.

"Si. The *demon rum!* Usually it's worse. Because of *Cinco de Mayo...*," Captain Lopez paused. "...Let's just say that Jean-Denis' gunplay earlier today put an end to their usual festivities..."

JJ cinched his purple sash. "And you?"

"Used to party until sunrise, right along with them. We were all *gypsies in the palace.*" Captain Lopez confessed. "But it doesn't compare to the adventures you've been on recently. That *Letter of Marque...*"

"Mr. Celi's *Letter of Marque?*" Zeke asked, turning his eyes toward the pirate captain.

"Cluck. cluck." A chicken scurried between Zeke's legs, followed by a fat pig. "Squeal. squeal."

"Fresh eggs...," Captain Lopez laughed. "...and bacon."

Isabella laughed at Zeke's shocked reaction. She turned to Juan Jon Lopez. "But what about the letter?"

"The challenges you've faced these past few days," Captain Lopez smiled. "They haven't been easy, but the three of you have proven to be resourceful, courageous, and spirited shipmates. Those qualities will serve you well..."

"What about the doubloon?" Isabella asked. "You put it in the well, didn't you?"

"I don't get around much these days. It was Jean-Denis who put it there," Captain Lopez nodded. "Had to get the journey started somehow..."

"Why didn't you just *pipe* us aboard the *GhostRider?*" JJ asked pointedly. "That's what the US Navy does..."

"You have to admit that, had it not been for the journey, none of you would have believed a single word I've told you." Captain Lopez smiled. "Besides, over the years I've found that experience is the best teacher..."

"But did you have to put us all in danger?" JJ asked, "just so you could talk to me?"

"It was your choice to bring your shipmates along. I had nothing to do with it." Captain Lopez waved an open hand. "But the only danger I see here, is in not learning any lessons from this adventure of yours..."

"My adventure?" JJ asked, exasperated. "It was the *Letter of Marque*..."

"As I recall, you're the one who always dreamed of such an adventure. Be careful what you ask for...you just might get it." Captain Lopez gave JJ a sly smile. "And as for the *Letter of Marque*, well, it was just a convenient way to make your dream happen..."

"So everything we've been through these past few days..." Isabella paused "you knew what was going to happen, *before* it happened?"

"Sí, sí. Everything except the end of the *Ice Age* period. You needed to see the cave drawings to solve the first mystery clue. But I only ordered my crewe to take you back to 1528. Instead..." Captain Lopez shook his head. "...they took you back to 1528 BC. None of us were even around back then. My crewe was never very good at following my instructions..."

JJ laughed at Captain Lopez. "So you saw history unfold?"

"Sí, was there in 1757 when the British named Egmont Key after the Second Earl of Egmont. Saw Captain William Bunce come through here in 1839." Captain Lopez smiled at Zeke. "You writing all this down?"

"Yes, Captain." Zeke smiled, then continued writing. "Every word..."

"Saw the Seminole Wars, the Great Gale of 1848..." He turned to JJ.

"...Did that boat come in handy?"

"It was you?" JJ shook his head, smiling. "You sent us the *Sherrod Edwards*?"

"Actually, it was Jean-Denis' idea." Captain Lopez laughed, then gave a serious look. "I even witnessed the Civil War...That was quite tragic..."

"What about Billy and Azaelia?" Isabella interrupted. "Did they make it to Cuba?"

"Safe and sound, I'm happy to report." Captain Lopez beamed. "Billy's a preacher and..."

"What about Victoria," JJ interrupted. "Did she ever make it to Key West?"

"Si. But her evil father followed her down to *The Keys*. That was a couple of years ago, 1870, I believe..." Captain Lopez frowned. "I was there in 1980 when the *Summit Venture* hit the Sunshine Skyway Bridge. Very tragic...but I'm getting ahead of myself."

"So what year are we in now?" JJ asked. "When do we get to go home?"

"In a few hours we'll sail out closer to Egmont Key," Captain Lopez smiled. "Then Jean-Denis will take you on the longboat. Put you ashore on the island..."

"What about you?" Isabella asked, concerned.

"Perhaps I will find a peaceful place to rest." He turned to JJ. "But that is up to you. The course you chart is your own..."

"Thanks." JJ's eyes welled with tears.

"There is nothing you can't do if you choose to believe." The pirate captain leaned into JJ. He whispered, "Yo Creo!"

"Ship ahoy, Captain Lopez." The sailor called down from the crow's nest. He had a spyglass pressed firmly against his eye. "Too dark to see, but it looks like a transport ship."

"Si. Very good," Captain Lopez answered with a smile. "Must be the *Vigilancia*. We're right on schedule for the year 1898."

A shooting star streaked across the midnight darkness, bursting into a thousand points of light.

Chapter Thirty Two

Pirate Prisoners
(1898)

America was at war with the Spanish, Jean-Denis warned. It was 1898, and the Americans were fighting for the independence of the Caribbean island of Cuba. Under the cover of night, as Captain Lopez promised, the Bayway Buccaneers were transported by longboat to Egmont Key. "Remember", Jean-Denis reminded them, "the course is yours to chart. But you must choose to believe". After bidding him farewell, the trio followed the beach toward the blinking lighthouse.

Tired and weary, they decided to rest for the night inside a small abandoned shelter that lay near the beach. Home, they agreed, could wait another day.

The trio planned to solve the sixth mystery clue first thing in the morning. Well-rested, they'd pass the lighthouse, and head toward the old fort to meet up with Mr. Celi and their classmates. Undoubtedly, they thought, everyone would be frantically searching for the trio. After being discovered, they'd rush to their friends, bragging about the journey on the Egmont Passage. Little did they know, however, that more adventure lay ahead before home would be within reach.

****

"Wake up! Wake up"

"What?" JJ asked, refusing to open his eyes. He yawned, then turned

99

on his side.

The humid, cloudless morning on Egmont Key was typical of summer in Florida. To the east, rising over Shell Key and a hundred other mangrove islands, the rising sun flashed a brilliant orange. Standing proud watch over the troops below, the Egmont lighthouse edged over the tops of the Cabbage Palms. In the distance, brown pelicans circled and dive-bombed into the Gulf of Mexico, preying on a breakfast of mullet and sea trout.

Old Glory, its 45 white stars embroidered on a field of blue, waved high above a wooden pole. The flag flew quietly, as if not wanting to disturb the glorious morning unfolding over the military camp. But the quiet of the morning was broken by the primal call of a wild animal.

Did you hear that?" Isabella whispered. She shook JJ and Zeke.

Roar! ·

"Sounds like a lion," Isabella shook them again. "Listen. It's coming from the stand of mangroves over there."

"You must be dreaming," Zeke said, straining to keep his eyes closed. "All I hear is some hammering. Aren't many lions on this ship."

"That's what I'm trying to tell you," Isabella insisted. "We're not on the GhostRider anymore."

JJ and Zeke shot up, rubbing their eyes to coax them open.

"Oh, gawd!" Zeke shouted. He pulled at the pirate clothes from the GhostRider. "Where are we?"

"Don't know," Isabella replied. "But keep your voice down. There's someone outside."

The mountain lion's roar echoed off the silver Gulf of Mexico.

"I hear it again!" Isabella said. "I'm not hearing things."

"Where do you suppose we are?" Zeke whispered, slipping on his black buckled pirate boots.

"Don't know," Isabella replied. She tied her curly hair in a topknot, then borrowed JJ's Tampa Bay Buccaneer cap to hide the tangled mess.

"They're speaking English. That's a good sign!" JJ smiled. He removed the purple sash from his waist, then placed it around his neck. He then took an inventory of his knapsack. Glasses. Binoculars. Field Guide...

"The doubloon," JJ shouted. "It's gone!"

"So is the Letter of Marque," Isabella cried. "It's gone too!"

"Oh, gawd," Zeke panicked. "Where could it be..."

The trio peeked through window of the wooden cell. Several dozen tents, placed in perfect rows, lined the open field. Soldiers, some gaunt, and yellow, slowly moved about. One group of men, in various stages of dressing, sat near an open campfire eating bacon and eggs. Gopher turtles, ignoring the bustle of activity from the Tenth Regiment, crawled across the campsite in search of breakfast.

A wide officer, his horse kicking up white dust, wended between the rows of hospital tents. Pulling hard on the reins, he brought the galloping stallion to a quick halt, then abruptly dismounted. The horse nearly stalled from the heavy weight .

"They awake yet?" His tone was harsh. The officer gave very little expression as he moved toward the prison cell.

"Yes, sir." Corporal Baggs leaped to attention, snapping a smart salute. "Been hearing some whispering for a while."

Lieutenant Dorfman wobbled past the corporal. He pushed the door hard, making a loud *bang* when it hit the wooden wall.

"Know why you're in the stockade?" His chubby jowls flapped with his words. "Been losing lots of stuff around this camp. Provisions, watches, wallets, jewelry. Even our mountain lion is missing. Took quite a bit of nerve to steal the regiment's mascot. It's the type of activity normally associated with *piracy*." He angrily emphasized the word *piracy*.

"But we're not pirates..." Isabella stammered apologetically.

"Tell it to Major Klearly. You can defend yourselves after his speech." Lieutenant Dorfman adjusted the Cuban cigar dangling on his lips. "Then we'll have the time to deal with you! Most people that steal from the US gov' ment are executed by a firing squad. Especially during times of war." He threw a newspaper at their feet, gave a sinister laugh, then wobbled out the cell.

"Bring 'em to the docks in an hour," Lieutenant Dorfman ordered. "Major Klearly will take 'em back to Tampa for a quick trial."

Chapter Thirty Three

The "Rough Riders"

"**What's** it say?" *Isabella and Zeke shouted as JJ rushed to pick up the folded newspaper.*

"It's the *West Hillsborough Times!*" *JJ read the banner at the top of the page.* "It's dated July, 4th, 1898!"

"We've flashed forward again!" *Zeke shook his head.* "Another twenty-six years!"

"But we're getting closer to home," *Isabella smiled optimistically.* "Read what it says, JJ."

JJ retrieved his reading glasses from the knapsack:

"'The Rough Riders, and the other soldiers fighting the Spanish-American War, are gaining ground on the Spanish army. Colonel Theodore Roosevelt and his band of men are making their way up San Juan Hill. Some months ago, these very same men mustered in the sleepy port of Tampa, preparing for their departure to the Caribbean island of Cuba. Aboard the USS Vigilancia...'"

"I remember studying about the *Rough Riders,*" *Isabella smiled.* "That Roosevelt. He sure was something..."

"'But it is the hot, wet Cuban summer, not the Spanish army, that is giving Roosevelt's men their toughest challenge.'" *JJ continued reading.* "'To the rear of the fighting, the dreaded 'yellow jack' flag hangs limply in the still air. It flies in an isolated camp, a sure sign that malaria had infested the men. One in five American soldiers is stricken with the 'yellow fever' and other diseases. The misery of the camp is a stark contrast to the brave fighting going on in San Juan Hill, Cuba...'"

"Geez." Isabella dropped her head. "Sounds quite horrible!"

"'...Before anyone can return home from the war in the Caribbean,'" JJ read, "most of the soldiers are expected to be quarantined for ten days on a remote island in the Gulf of Mexico...'"

"Sounds like it's not much of a picnic down there," Zeke shook his head.

"I wonder what island they're talking about?" JJ looked up from the newspaper. "I'll look it up in my book..."

Corporal Baggs knocked once, opening the cell door. "Excuse me," he said, absent of emotion, "I have orders to take you down to the docks."

Chapter Thirty Four

I Can See Klearly

Major Henry Klearly, well-groomed and stiff, sat in the bridge of the *USS Verdad* as it steamed out through the mouth of Tampa Bay. Having been asked to address the artillery troops on Egmont Key, he sat quietly reviewing his Independence Day speech for America's 122nd birthday. Because of the war, patriotism ran hard and deep.

Despite his personal feelings, his speech would be morale-boosting, he decided. Major Klearly fought pangs of anger that he and his troops were missing the action in the Caribbean. Instead, he sat on the sidelines in mosquito-infested Tampa, waiting out the war.

The pilot steered the boat toward the dock below the rebuilt Egmont Lighthouse. Artillery cannons, their barrels aimed toward the gulf, stood watch over Tampa Bay. The soldiers had no way of knowing they would never engage in combat with the Spanish armada.

As the boat slowed for its approach on the wooden dock, Major Klearly, tall and thin, carefully folded his speech and placed it in his shirt pocket. Looking up for the first time, he noticed a short squatty officer standing at attention, a cigar dangling on his lip. Standing next to the him was a young corporal, and three pirate prisoners.

"Good morning, Major Klearly. The men are looking forward to your speech!" Lieutenant Dorfman smiled, giving a sloppy salute. Then turning toward the Bayway Buccaneers said, "These are the prisoners I wired you about last night."

"They're just kids," Major Klearly shot back.

"Lots of stuff's been missing around here, sir." The lieutenant dropped his salute. "We figure these pirates have something to do with the Egmont Key thefts..."

"We're not pirates," Isabella insisted."

"Hush, young lady." Lieutenant Dorfman snarled, showing his pointed brown teeth.

"Don't look too dangerous to me," Major Klearly answered. "Let them speak."

"Sir," JJ stepped forward. "We've been on quite a long journey and..."

Major Klearly stared deeply into JJ's eyes, as if searching for something. He turned, staring into Isabella's eyes, then Zeke's.

"...I believe these *pirates* have something to do with the thefts." Lieutenant Dorfman interrupted, shifting the cigar in his mouth. "They may even be spies. Take a look at this! It's a *Letter of Marque* with a map of the islands. And it mentions something about some places I never even heard of before. Has some sort of secret code on the back. Take a look at the last line..."

Major Klearly read the sixth clue. *This future president traveled through Tampa Bay on his way to fight in the Spanish-American War.*

"What do you have to say for yourselves?" Major Klearly asked, reading the *Letter of Marque* in his hand.

"Well, sir," JJ answered bravely. "we haven't stolen anything from you."

"Nothing at all," Isabella agreed. "And we're not spies, either."

"We're just trying to get back home," Zeke added. "And that's the truth."

"And where might that be?" Major Klearly asked.

"It's a long story, sir. But it's over there, on the mainland. And that *Letter of Marque*, it's not real." Isabella took a moment to collect her thoughts. "It's just a school project we've been working on."

"Tell me about this journey of yours. What have you learned?"

"Well, we've learned lots about history. Like the explorers, and the Civil War..." Zeke answered.

"And we learned that people can be trusted and..." Isabella continued.

"Major Klearly..." JJ interrupted, clearing his throat. "...Above all, we've learned that life is a journey...and even though there might be some challenges...we should still take the time to enjoy all of it..."

"I see." Henry Klearly jotted a quick note on a piece of scrap paper, then handed it to Corporal Baggs. "Here," He said impatiently. "wire this note back to my Tampa headquarters. I want a quick response."

Leaving his pirate prisoners behind in the charge of Corporal Baggs, Lieutenant Dorfman escorted Major Klearly down the shell path. White limestone powder stirred under the weight of the lieutenant's feet. Turning around to Baggs, the lieutenant barked, "Chain 'em to the docks until after the speech. If they cause you any trouble..."

"Hold on there, lieutenant," Major Klearly said abruptly. "Don't you think you're being a bit too harsh on these kids?"

"Well no, sir...." The lieutenant stammered.

"The fact is, you don't know who's been stealing from you." Major Klearly adjusted the gig line on his belt. Then, peering angrily into Lieutenant Dorfman's eyes, he said, "You have no proof. Isn't that right?"

"Well, sir..." The lieutenant choked back his Cuban stogie.

"Well what?" Major Klearly shot back in anger. "We'll take the kids with us."

Lieutenant Dorfman wobbled back to retrieve the three prisoners.

"I'll keep a watchful eye on them," Major Klearly shouted. "Get them some clothes, too. Can't have my guests dressed as pirates for America's birthday celebration."

****

The scurry of busy soldiers, who had looked like army ants building a dirt pile, was replaced with eager anticipation. Their hammers and saws put away, they had changed into clean uniforms and now sat on the wooden benches in front of the grandstand where Major Henry Klearly would deliver his speech. Red, white, and blue bunting covering the front of the stand, ruffled in the summer breeze. To the back of the island, in sharp contrast to the 4th of July celebration, the *Yellow Jack* hung low on the flag pole over an isolated group of tents from Hospital Regiment B.

****

The four-man brass band bellowed *Stars and Stripes Forever* upon Major Klearly's arrival on the grandstand. The band played off-key, but nobody noticed. To Lieutenant Dorfman's chagrin, he was ordered to add three additional chairs on the platform. Major Klearly sat in the first chair, followed by JJ, Isabella, and Zeke. Lieutenant Dorfman sat on the end.

The color guard marched in, stepping to the beat of a sour rendition of *My Country 'Tis Of Thee.*

From the podium, the chaplain asked for blessings upon all Americans. Then, bowing his head, he asked for special blessings for the men fighting the war against Spain, and for the Red Cross ladies led by Clara Barton. They were doing "God's" work, he said.

The Egmont Light keeper spoke next. He said the Egmont Lighthouse was a beacon of hope, and that he was proud to have the brave men of the artillery battery on his island. The light keeper then introduced Lieutenant Dorfman.

Lieutenant Dorfman rambled for nearly 20-minutes, giving a year-by-year account, beginning in 1776, of America's 122-year history. The lieutenant was up to the *Battle of Gettysburg*, when Corporal Baggs rushed up the grandstand with a telegram in his hand. Tripping on the last step, the private skidded on his belly across the platform. Too focused on his isolated moment of glory, Lieutenant Dorfman continued with his speech, failing to notice the corporal's grand entrance, and the resultant laughter from the crowd.

Corporal Baggs' skid stopped him short of Major Klearly's feet. Embarrassed, but remaining serious, he looked up to Major Klearly. "Two cables for you, sir," he whispered. "Both seem to be quite urgent."

Major Klearly read the first telegram. It was from the War Department in Washington, DC

After another ten minutes passed, Lieutenant Dorfman relinquished the podium to his commander. Although quite uninspiring, the lieutenant's lengthy speech gave Henry Klearly time to rewrite his own speech.

Major Klearly stepped to the podium to the sound of roaring applause. "It is a great privilege and honor to speak before you on this day, America's 122 birthday..."

Major Henry Klearly's polished brass glimmered in the soft morning sun as he read his speech:

"...The legacy of our nation's military has long been that of courage, bravery, and uncommon valor.....The road to heroism is often unplanned, and is often traveled by ordinary men in extraordinary circumstances. Men just like you, here on Egmont Key, protecting Tampa Bay from the Spanish armada. And like the American soldiers in Cuba, fighting to liberate the people from the tyranny of the Spanish crown...."

The teenagers sat in awed silence as American history unfolded before their eyes.

"...Moments ago I was handed a cable from Washington, D.C." Major Klearly smiled at Corporal Baggs who had taken his seat in the audience.

"The dateline was yesterday, July 3, 1898." Henry Klearly retrieved the telegram from his shirt pocket:

"Colonel Teddy Roosevelt and the Rough Riders have taken control of San Juan Hill. We expect imminent liberation of Cuba, followed by surrender of war from Spain..."

"The war is over," shouted the crowd of soldiers, throwing their hats in the air. Tears of joy filled their eyes. Flags waved in the hands of the triumphant soldiers.

"But our work here is not done," Major Klearly continued, wiping the moisture from his eyes. "At least not yet..."

"...Prepare for a mission change. Coastal batteries will remain operational until further notice. Prepare to convert Egmont Key to a hospital quarantine station. Expect to build a 1,000 tent city for the returning soldiers from Cuba. More details to follow. Signed, Secretary of War.

The soldiers roared to life again. The four-man band played a jubilant version of *When Johnny Comes Marching Home*, with the crowd instinctively singing along.

Major Klearly continued with his speech, waving his arms in the air:

"Let me conclude by saying, that although the war is not quite yet over, America appreciates your uncommon courage, bravery and valor, and like the men of Roosevelt's Rough Rider brigade...

"... Let the light shining before us," Henry Klearly looked up at the flashing lighthouse. "Let it be the pilot light that guides the safe return home of all the men fighting in the Caribbean. God bless you. And Happy Birthday America..."

The crowd roared to life a final time, as the teenagers followed Major Klearly down the steps of the grandstand.

"Lieutenant Dorfman," Major Klearly shouted above the noise of the crowd. "I need to speak with you."

Seven coastal cannons, aimed at an unseen enemy, fired a volley of three shots across the turquoise gulf waters. Twenty-one guns saluted the war's end.

Chapter Thirty Five

"It's In The Eyes"

Following the speech, Major Klearly gave JJ, Zeke, and Isabella the freedom to move about the Egmont Camp. When evening dawned, Henry Klearly invited them to a private dinner in his command tent.

"Too much celebration going on in the junior officers' mess tent. They've wet down the counter with their cider." Major Klearly shook his head smiling. "They're sliding across the counter in full dress uniform. Calling them *carrier landings*. Not sure exactly what that is."

"Thanks for your hospitality, sir," Isabella said politely. The teenagers sat at a private table, dining on roast beef with horse radish sauce, with a side of corn-on-the cob and muffin bread. "We had a great day!"

"Glad you had a nice time," Major Klearly said. "I was hoping it would sort of make up for spending the night in that cold stockade..."

"We've had worse nights than that jail," JJ smiled, remembering the *Gale of 1848* beneath the *Sherrod Edwards* . "At least the jail was dry."

"Did you really think we were spies?" Zeke asked, wiping horse radish from his chin. "Like Dorfman said we were..."

"Lieutenant Dorfman," Major Klearly gave a faint smile. "You won't be seeing him for a while. As of this moment, he and some of his men are locked up in that very same stockade you were in last night..."

"Was wondering where he went after the ceremony." Isabella sipped apple cider from a tin cup. "Please forgive me for saying this, but he's not a very good leader..."

"No need to apologize." He chuckled at her candor. "I've had my eye on Dorfman for quite a while. The thieving around this camp is legendary....long before you arrived..."

"So you believed us?" Zeke cut into the prime rib.

"Sure. I pride myself on being a good judge of character." Henry Klearly smiled. "Otherwise I wouldn't have let you freely roam the camp."

"Then how did you know that Dorfman was involved with the Egmont Key thefts?" JJ plucked a kernel of corn from his front teeth.

"I had Corporal Baggs send a cable to Tampa," Major Klearly continued. "And then at the ceremony this morning I received two cables in return. The first one, as you know, was from DC, announcing victory on San Juan Hill..."

"And the second one?" Isabella asked.

"The second was a reply to my cable." Major Klearly answered. "It was from Tampa. Apparently Dorfman and a couple of others are involved in some sort of scam."

"A scam?" Isabella asked.

"That's right!" Major Klearly shook his head, disbelieving. "And your arrival was a convenient way for him to put the blame on someone else..."

"But how did you know to question Dorfman's story?" JJ listened intently, hanging on his every word.

"Quite unusual, really," Major Klearly answered, still perplexed. "Before I left Tampa...for the speech...I received an unexpected visitor..."

"What was his name?" JJ leaned toward Major Klearly. "Did he give his name?"

"No, sir," Major Klearly answered politely. "But he did say that he had information regarding the stolen items on Egmont Key. He knew about the three of you..."

"He knew about us being taken prisoner?" Isabella questioned.

"No one was supposed to know about your being taken prisoner." Major Klearly smoothed the linen napkin on his lap. "But the man asked me to judge for myself before pursuing the matter of piracy before the Judge Advocate General..."

"Why would this guy even care about us?" Zeke shook his head. He pulled out his notepad. "Mind if I takes some notes?"

"Go right ahead...I don't know why the man would be interested in you." Major Klearly shrugged. "But he said, in order for me to get the much needed information about the Egmont Key thefts...he needed me to get some information from you..."

"From us?" JJ pulled his head back, clearly confused. "But we know nothing about the thefts..."

"No. It's not like that at all." Major Klearly smiled. "In exchange for the information, all I had to do was ask you about your journey..."

"He wanted information about our journey?" Isabella asked. "I don't get it..."

"I know. It was quite an unusual request. But the question was worth asking. I had to get the information to bust Dorfman." Major Klearly frowned. "So before the ceremony this morning, I cabled the man back at my Tampa headquarters. Gave him your answer to his question..."

"What was his reply? Zeke asked, making a note in his pad.

"Here, read it for yourself." Henry Klearly handed the cable to Zeke.

Major Klearly,
    Glad to learn my shipmates have learned to make the best of their journey. Please remind them there is still one more mystery clue to solve. And only then will their journey end where it began. Only then will they be allowed to go home.
    As for the information you are seeking on the Egmont Key thefts, ask Lieutenant Dorfman about the buried loot at the foot of the Egmont Lighthouse.
                                    Regards, a friend

"Didn't know what to make of the cable at first. But after the ceremony, Dorfman and I paid a visit to the lighthouse. After we did a little digging he confessed to the whole thing..." Henry Klearly shook his head, disgusted. "It was all right there, just as the mystery visitor said it would be. Jewelry. Money. Even camp supplies..."

"So Lieutenant Dorfman admitted that we were never involved?" JJ asked.

"Actually, quite the opposite." Major Klearly shook his head. "He said you were part of the scheme..."

"But that's not true at all..." Zeke shot back defensively.

"Oh, I know." Major Klearly chuckled, putting a calm hand on Zeke's shoulder. "He was just trying to spread the blame around..."

"So you determined our guilt or innocence based on our answer to the mystery man's question?" Isabella gave Major Klearly a bewildered look.

"Not at all," Henry Klearly shook his head. "That wasn't part of the agreement..."

"So how did you decide we were telling the truth?" JJ asked.

"It's in the eyes. They are the window to the soul." He cut into the prime rib, then looked at JJ. "Back at the dock...After I looked each of you directly in the eyes. Well, I knew right away you kids had no part of the Egmont Key thefts..."

"Really?" JJ smiled broadly.

"What about the mountain lion?" Isabella dipped the last bite of prime rib into the horse radish. "How'd it get loose?"

"That lion is our mascot," Major Klearly dismissed the thought. "It kept getting loose over in Tampa, so we brought it over to the island thinking it would be safer..."

"Awesome," Zeke shouted. "So all the charges have been dropped?"

"Actually, you've been free to go all day." Henry Klearly smiled. "My men have cots set up for you in one of our guest tents. You'll find all your belongings there. Including your *Letter of Marque*."

"Thank you for dinner." Isabella walked around the table. She gave Henry Klearly a big hug, then pecked him on the check. "It was quite the best. And so are you."

Zeke reached across the dinner table, giving Major Klearly a firm handshake. Klearly's thin hands felt stronger than they appeared.

"Found this gold coin in Dorfman's possession." Major Klearly said, turning to JJ. "Feel certain it belongs to you..."

Excusing himself from the dinner table, Henry Klearly walked toward the open tent flap. Then, turning back toward his guests, he said, "I don't know what to make of your game. But the answer to the last mystery clue is *Teddy Roosevelt*...I've met him a few times. He's a man destined for greatness...."

"Theodore Roosevelt?" JJ repeated.

"Sure. I'm a good judge of character." He gave them a wink. "That's what I told the Frenchman."

Chapter Thirty Six

"Someone Special"

The Bayway Buccaneers retired to the comforts of their cots in Major Henry Klearly's guest tent. A kerosene lamp hung from the center pole, its light casting long shadows on the canvas panels.

"Ezekiel," Isabella said affectionately, "mind if I borrow your pad and pen?"

"Nah. Go right ahead." Zeke slid his body between the two thin US Army blankets. He closed his eyes whispering, "It's been quite an adventure. Can't wait to start writing this story..."

"Yeah. It's been a heck of a journey." JJ squeezed the doubloon in his

hand. "Maybe tomorrow we'll be home," he added, before falling fast asleep.

Isabella sat on the cot with her eyes fixed on JJ. She wondered what Captain Lopez had told him during their private conversation the night before. *What impact would the pirate captain's words have on JJ,* she thought. Isabella's eyes glistened in the lamplight as she carefully penned a note to Henry Klearly. She reread the note, then smiled as her eyes drifted up toward JJ.

Dear Major Klearly,

I, too, have the wonderful feeling of knowing someone special before they have discovered it for themselves. The Teddy Bear is yours in appreciation for all your help.

Sincerely, Isabella

She folded the note, then quietly walked across the tent, placing the stuffed bear and note next to the open flap. Returning next to JJ, she softly kissed him on the cheek.

"*Yo Creo,*" Isabella whispered, looking at the coin held loosely in JJ's hand.

Outside the tent, brilliant fireworks flashed red, white, and blue in the clear skies over Egmont Key, the patriotic colors mirrored on the waters of the Gulf of Mexico.

Chapter Thirty Seven

Kermit The Hermit

The Bayway Buccaneers awoke beneath the broad limbs of a Gumbo Limbo tree. Although late 20th Century Florida brought crowded cities, highways, high rises, and pollution, modern technology had yet to change the natural beauty of Florida's Gulf Coast.

The full moon, its light dancing on the waves like shimmering diamonds, began its descent over the western horizon. Sailboats, still lit in reds and greens from the Tierra Verde boat parade, bobbed at anchor in the open bay. The familiar sound of a holiday tune played from the cabin of a nearby sailboat.

"...I'll be home for Christmas, you can count on me..."

"Wake up! Wake up!"

"Listen," Isabella squeezed JJ's shoulder, trying to shake him awake. Her pleas were ignored. "It's a Christmas carol."

"Lemme sleep, Izzy." JJ rolled over on the sand, covering his eyes with his shirt.

"Zeke, wake up. Listen," Isabella whispered. "Do you hear it?"

"Yeah, I hear it." He yawned, then sat up, rubbing the sleep from his eyes. "Where's it coming from?"

"I think from that sailboat," she pointed to the horizon. "Over there near Cabbage Key."

"I guess we're not with Major Klearly anymore," JJ groaned a matter-of-fact tone. He rose from his sleep, flattening the wrinkles from his *britches.*

"I'll be home for Christmas, if only in my dreams..."

The sixth mystery clue, solved by Major Henry Klearly the night before, gave the trio new hope for returning home safely. With renewed optimism, the trio gathered their belongings, heading toward Old Fort Dade on the eastern shore of Egmont Key.

The sun, rising over the Sunshine Skyway Bridge, gave chase to the falling moon. Closer in, on Fort DeSoto, a large American flag with 50 stars, waved majestically over the new morning.

"...48, 49, 50," JJ lowered his binoculars and smiled. "Can't tell for sure. You take a look."

Zeke focused the binoculars on the flag. "Yup. Looks like there are fifty stars on it."

"Maybe we're home," Isabella shouted enthusiastically.

Their pace increased as they marched along the leeward shore. Stopping only once, at a large metal object buried deeply in the wet sand.

"What do you think it is?" Zeke examined the camouflaged brown and green paint. "Looks like parts of some plane! Been here a while though."

"Yeah. Looks like a wing." Isabella brushed sand off the metal surface. "Hey guys, look at these markings!"

"I'll bet it's part of an F-4," JJ decided. "Look at the camouflaged markings."

"Yeah," Zeke recalled. "They use to fly these fighters at MacDill Air Force Base in the 1980's. I'll bet some fighter-jock ditched it in the gulf!"

"Maybe a storm just washed it on shore?" Isabella suggested.

Zeke cleared the wet sand off the wing of the downed fighter jet. JJ, leaning his hand on the surviving landing gear, looked for more evidence from the plane.

"Major Klearly gave us the answer to the last clue," Isabella said, unfolding the *Letter of Marque* across the metal wing. "He said it was *Theodore Roosevelt.*"

"But do the letters fit in the blank spaces?" Zeke sat on the wing, craning his neck in Isabella's direction.

"Nah," she said disappointedly. "*Roosevelt* fits. But not *Theodore.*"

"What about *Teddy,*" JJ asked, pointing his index finger toward the open pages of his field guide. "Says here that *Teddy* Roosevelt was the 26th president. Izzy, see if *T-E-D-D-Y* fits!"

Isabella mouthed the letters as she ran her finger across the blank spaces for the last clue. "It fits," Isabella screamed. "We solved the sixth mystery clue. It fits!" She tossed the *Letter of Marque* in the air. It fell gently to the moist sand. Isabella danced in circles around the map, lying on the white beach.

JJ and Zeke followed Isabella's lead. They danced in circles, kicking, sand in the air with their bare feet. They flapped their arms in a joyous frenzy.

"It fits," JJ chanted, tossing his *Buccaneer* hat in the air. "It fits."

"*Teddy fits*," Zeke shouted, circling around Isabella. "He fits."

Down the beach, a few hundred feet away, a stranger watched the Bayway Buccaneers in great amusement. He walked closer along the shoreline, nearing the celebration.

"*Teddy fits! Teddy fits!*" they chanted. "*Teddy fits...*"

"You kids okay?" the stranger asked. The soft morning light revealed a weathered face of an old man. He was dressed in faded swim trunks, leather sandals, and a threadbare T-shirt. Noticing he had startled the trio, he added, "I'm sorry, didn't mean to scare you."

"Just having a little fun," Zeke answered defensively. He was guarded with his words. "Nothing wrong with that, is there?"

"We just learned some good news, that's all." JJ interrupted Zeke, giving a more friendly tone to the conversation. He waved the letter in the air.

"Quite some celebration there. I believe in having fun, too." The stranger gave a toothless smile. He was short and thin, with broad round eyes and an oversized nose. "My name's Kermit. People call me *Kermit the Hermit*."

"Hi, I'm JJ." He picked up his Buccaneer cap, placed it back on his head. "This is Zeke, and Isabella."

Isabella offered her hand to Kermit. A brown creature, its body elongated and furry, scurried up the old man's T-shirt, then crawled inside through the collar. It popped its chipmunk-like face out of Kermit's shirt sleeve. "What's that?" she shrieked, pulling her hand back.

"Don't mind him," Kermit chuckled, rubbing the back of the ferret's head with his scarred fingers. "This is Calypso. He's just showing off."

Isabella made quick friends with Calypso. The ferret sat on her shoulder as the trio continued their conversation.

"Cheep, cheep." Calypso made a rat's nest out of Isabella's curly hair. The creature leaped onto Zeke's *Gator* cap, then hopscotched onto JJ's shoulder. He scurried down his shirt and into one of JJ's pockets.

"Cheep, cheep," he said softly. Calypso stirred a while before falling *fast asleep in JJ's pocket.*

"Calypso," Kermit said admonishingly. "Please excuse his forwardness. He's not used to being around other people."

"I don't mind at all. He's already sleeping." JJ pointed to Kermit's thin chest. "I like your shirt..."

Kermit looked down at the words on his faded T-shirt, *Life Is A Journey, Make Fun Of It.* "I love it too." He gave another toothless smile. "It was my abuela's favorite saying! I wear the shirt all the time."

"It's a truism." JJ smiled, changing the subject. "Don't suppose you saw anyone this early in the morning?"

"Haven't seen anyone yet," Kermit answered. "Except for the cruise lines, not many merchant ships are passing through the bay. That means there's not much need for the Egmont harbor pilots. So they've all gone home for the holidays. You should do the same..."

Isabella gave him a disappointed look. "We thought some of our friends might be there to meet us at Fort Dade."

"You sure?" Kermit gave her a puzzled look. "It's Christmas Eve."

"Christmas Eve?" Zeke asked.

"Won't be too many people visiting the island today. Besides...." he paused a moment. "Except for the archeologists from the Preservation Society, Fort Dade's been closed off to the public for quite some time."

"That can't be," Zeke said sadly. "You sure?"

"It's true," Kermit apologized. "Back in 1985, Hurricane Elena, some of the other storms too. They nearly destroyed the old fort. The Preservation Society is trying to restore it now."

"But that fort," Isabella wiped away a tear, "it's our only way home!"

"Look, I know it's none of my business," Kermit said genuinely. "I'm just an old Conch from Key West..."

"Key West?" JJ smiled. "We have a friend down there from way back..."

"You wouldn't have wanted me for your friend back then. Had to leave *The Keys* in a real hurry, if you know what I mean. So I know what it's like being on the run. Know what it's like to be homeless, too. If there's anyway I can help...."

"We're not on the run." Zeke struggled to hold back his disappointment. "And we're not exactly homeless..."

"But you have no idea what we've gone through just to get here," JJ said sadly. "We've been following the beacon from the lighthouse, hoping it would lead us to old Fort Dade..."

"You know," *Kermit the Hermit* grinned. "You should check the small

118

things in your letter..."

"*How'd you know about the....You're right, Kermit! Sometimes the answers are in the details. We'll keep that in mind.*" Isabella frowned, thinking about her classmates. "*It's just that we thought our friends would be looking for us at the fort. And now you say that it's been destroyed by some storm.*"

"*I said nearly destroyed,*" Kermit gently corrected her. "*Oh, it's still there. The fort wasn't used much after WW I. It just sat there decaying in the summer heat and salt air. And over the years the hurricanes destroyed some of the artillery batteries. Washed them clear away into the Gulf of Mexico. Now, much of the fort is covered with sand.*"

"*Covered with sand?*" JJ said incredulously.

"*The archeologists from the society,*" Kermit pointed toward the northern part of the island, "*they don't know what they'll find beneath the sand once they dig it out. But the fort's still there.*"

"*Think anyone will be there this morning?*" Isabella asked hopefully.

"*I'm not so sure,*" Kermit answered. "*being that it's Christmas Eve. Don't know if anyone will be working today.*"

"*I think he's awake,*" JJ reached in his pocket, retrieving Calypso.

"*He loves taking walks,*" Kermit chuckled. He took the ferret from JJ, placing him in a burlap pouch. "*But gets sleepy when I stop. I suppose we better get going.*"

"*Thanks, Kermit,*" JJ shook his hand. "*You've been very helpful.*"

"*Don't give up hope. I'm sure you'll find your friends somewhere.*" Kermit resumed his walk on the beach. "*Merry Christmas.*"

"*Merry Christmas,*" the teenagers shouted.

Kermit walked a few steps, then turned around on the beach toward the teenagers. "*Yo Creo.*"

"*What did you say?*" Isabella asked.

"*Is this yours?*" Kermit said holding up a gold coin. "*Found it in Calypso's pouch. Ferrets are natural born thieves. I'm sorry, but he really doesn't know any better. He must have stolen it from your pocket.*"

"*Thanks, Kermit,*" JJ returned the doubloon to the pocket in his cargo shorts.

"*Many years ago when I lived in Key West,*" Kermit paused to recall his memory. "*It was my abuela's house...*

"*What's an abuela?*" Isabella asked inquisitively.

"*Oh, that means grandmother in Spanish.*" Kermit smiled. "*My abuela lived on the corner of Begin and End, down on highway US 1. That's* where I met someone who showed me a coin with the same words..."

"Really," Zeke said. "JJ found the doubloon at Fort DeSoto."

"The man I met was actually quite wise." Kermit shook his head. "Looking back, he seemed to know a lot about the future. But I chose to ignore his advice to chart my own course in life..."

"Yo Creo." Isabella interrupted. "What does it mean?"

"It means *I believe*," Kermit answered.

"*I believe?* That's what it means?" JJ whispered, shaking his head. "Well that's quite simple. I thought it would have had a more mysterious meaning than that...."

"Do you remember the man's name?" Isabella asked hopefully.

"No. Don't recall the old salt's name." Calypso stirred in Kermit's pouch. "Okay, Calypso, we'll go home and get your breakfast. It was nice meeting you kids. Merry Christmas..."

Kermit turned toward the beach, walking its edge. He turned one final time toward the teenagers, who had already started their walk in the opposite direction.

"GhostRider," Kermit said in a low voice. "Don't recall the man's name. But I remember abuela Victoria saying the man sailed on a ship called the GhostRider."

An F-4 fighter jet streaked across the morning sky, drowning out *Kermit the Hermits* final words.

Chapter Thirty Eight

Old Fort Dade
(1996)

The trio passed the Egmont Lighthouse on their way to old Fort Dade. As Kermit stated, the fort was covered with a 15 foot sand dune. With the exception of a few loyal archeologists, the fort was barren.

The portable radio, sitting on the wall next to one of the diggers, blared out a song:

'...*The waterfront is reveling, the season has begun*
A sailor spends his Christmas in a harbor having fun...'

"*...from Jimmy Buffet's new CD, A Sailor's Christmas.*" The DJ interrupted the end of the song to deliver the holiday forecast. "*Today's weather will be clear and sunny, high temperature about 71 degrees...*"

The teenagers scanned the fort and the handful of preservation workers.

"Incredible." JJ scanned the walls of the fort. "Looks like a scene from an *Indiana Jones* movie."

An archeologist, his pith helmet drenched in sweat, adjusted his khaki shorts. He stabbed his shovel deep in the coarse sand, scooping the contents into a small wheel barrel.

"May I help you?" the digger asked, as he continued working the shovel.

"We're just looking for some friends..." Isabella replied.

The digger waved his hand, as if stopping traffic. He turned the volume up on the portable radio, cocking his ear toward the tiny speaker.

"*In local news...*" the reporter read the script in front of him. "*the city of Saint*

Petersburg continues to feel the effects of the recent riots in south Saint Petersburg. Last month's grand jury decision..."

"Please excuse me," he said. "Things are tense in the city right now. I was hoping the holidays would help bring a little peace to our community. It's quite tragic about those street riots."

"Street riots?" Zeke asked.

"Sure. You haven't heard about the *disturbances* in St. Petersburg? It's made national news. A white cop killed a black teenager. The whole south side of town erupted in riots and fires." He shook his head in disgust. "The governor had to declare a state of emergency. Where have you kids been?"

"Been away for a while," JJ answered quickly. "We're just now getting home."

"Hopefully something good will come out of all the destruction. I honestly thought we were beyond all this." He shook his head again, this time in disbelief. "Hopefully 1997 will be a better year..."

"1997? A better year?" Isabella turned to Zeke and JJ, whispering, "we're not home yet?"

"You were saying something about meeting friends here," the digger interrupted.

"Oh right. Our friends...." Isabella cleared her head. "They were suppose to meet us here after a field trip."

"Field trip? It's not a school day. And no one's been here all morning." The digger untied the scarf on his neck, wiping the sweat from his tanned face. Resting his arms on a shovel, he said, "But the area has been restricted for quite some time. So I wouldn't expect too many visitors here."

"Yeah, we know." JJ answered. "Kermit told us Fort Dade would be closed."

"Kermit?" the digger questioned.

"Kermit the Hermit said he lived here on Egmont Key," JJ answered.

"Besides the ship pilots," the digger replied, "no one has lived on the island for quite some time."

"Well," Isabella asked, "do you mind if we take a quick look around anyway?"

"Make it quick," the digger kicked the sand off his shovel with his brown boots. "It's the holidays, remember. We'll be leaving early and won't be back until after the new year. Wouldn't want anyone wandering around without supervision. Can be a bit dangerous out here."

"...In sports news, the University of Florida Gators are trying to bounce back

122

from their recent loss to the Florida State Seminoles. The 'Noles are predicted to win the National Championship in a rematch with the Gators in New Orleans on January 2. In other sports news, the Tampa Bay Buccaneers..."

The digger reached over to the radio and clicked it off. "I wish the Buccaneers were as successful as our college teams. Heck, I'd be happy if they could just make it to the playoffs. Can't believe they only won 6 games this year..."

"Keep the faith. The *Buccaneers*," Zeke smiled, "they'll win big someday!"

"What?" The digger asked.

"We're big *Bucs* fans, too," JJ grinned. "Call it an early Christmas present, but someday our *Buccaneers* will beat the *Oakland Raiders* in their first *Super Bowl...*"

"You're kidding..," the digger shook his head in disbelief.

"I predict...," Zeke smiled at JJ, then at the digger, "the score will be *48-21...*"

"We better get going," Isabella smiled, changing the subject. "Merry Christmas."

The trio headed around the main mortar pit, away from where the archeologists were digging. Through the thicket of palms and brush, they saw an old artillery battery that had been washed into the Gulf of Mexico.

"Hey kids," the digger turned the corner, chasing after the teenagers. "Forgot to mention something to you. Be careful near that artesian well we just uncovered. Could be quite dangerous if you fall in."

Chapter Thirty Nine

The Seventh Mystery

Isabella sat on an old artillery battery half submerged by high tide. Zeke sitting next to her, thumbed through the pages of his travel journal.

"I don't understand it," JJ shook his head, leafing through his field guide.

"Me neither. It just doesn't make any sense." Isabella frowned, nearly in tears. She unfolded Mr. Celi's *Letter of Marque*, flipping it from one side to the other. She looked at the map, then the mystery clues, and back again. "We wasted hours combing the area, and I've checked the details, just like Kermit suggested..."

"And we're a week away from the year 1997," Zeke sighed, shaking his head. "Yet we're still seven years from home," his voice trailed, "so close, and yet..."

"Come on guys. Let's not give up now." JJ hopped off the short wall and turned toward his friends. "We've gone through all sorts of stuff together. Let's not give up hope. There has gotta to be some simple explanation. Something's missing," he said confidently. "Let's go through the clues one more time..."

"But we've already checked the details. Rechecked them, too," Isabella slapped the letter in frustration.

"Let's just look at it one more time," JJ pleaded. "Please, just one more time."

"'Clue 1,'" Isabella read the *Letter of Marque*: "'This prehistoric Florida mammal is not in the canine family...'"

"*Saber Tooth*," Zeke answered. "That's right."

Isabella reluctantly read the other clues. "...and *Clue 4*: He was the first to keep watch over this..."

"Yup. It's *Sherrod Edwards*," Zeke verified, scanning the pages of his journal for additional information. "Got it down right here. On our way to his camp Billy Barefoot told us how Mr. Edwards was the first lighthouse keeper of the Egmont Lighthouse."

"Yeah," JJ nodded in agreement. "I remember. It was just after the Great Gale of 1848."

"Seems just like yesterday," Isabella smiled, straining to see the humor. Reading the next clue she said, *Robert E. Lee*. I know that one's right. I figured that one out myself."

"And the last answer is *Teddy Roosevelt*." Zeke was disappointed. "Isabella is right. This is a waste of time. We're no better off now than..."

"Okay, okay," JJ said, maintaining the optimism. "The clues got us this far, but not quite far enough. We're close but there..."

"But what," Isabella interrupted. "But we're not close enough..."

"What I was going to say, Izzy," JJ paused a moment. "There has to be another answer that will take us the rest of the way home."

"I think it's another one of *Nasty Juan's* challenges," Zeke said. "We're doomed to be stuck in the 1990's."

"Maybe. But I don't think so." JJ took a long pause to collect his thoughts. "Remember when Mr. Celi took us to the *Salvadore Dali* museum last year?"

"Yeah." Isabella laughed. "When you guys got locked in the bathroom for the night?"

"Sure. The art museum in downtown St. Petersburg," Zeke asked. "How can I forget that? So what's that got to do with all this?"

"Zeke's right," Isabella said pointedly. "What does *Salvador Dali* have to do with getting us home?"

"Nothing at all," JJ replied. "But do you remember Dali's painting of Christopher Columbus?"

"Yeah. It was called *The Dreams of Christopher Columbus*," Isabella recalled.

"Right," JJ agreed. "When you first look at it, all you see a portrait of Christopher Columbus. Right?."

"But after a closer look," Isabella interrupted. "You see other stuff that you didn't know was there."

"So, are you saying there might be another clue, within the clues?" Zeke asked. "Like a seventh mystery clue?"

"Maybe so," JJ nodded his head. "Sometimes things aren't what they seem to be at all."

"Let's put all the answers together," Isabella said.

Zeke turned to a blank page in his journal. He listed the answers, one below the other:

1. **S a b e r   T o o t h**

2. **T o c   o b a g a s**

3. **P a n f i l o D e N a r v a e z**

4. *S h e r r o d E d w a r d s*

5. **R o b e r t E L e e**

6. **T e d d y   R o o s e v e l t**

"See any hidden clues yet?" Zeke asked hopefully.

"Not yet," Isabella answered.

"But keep going," JJ encouraged. "Scramble the words around."

Zeke wrote the words down backwards, listed them in reverse order. "Nothing," he said disappointedly. "Now what?"

"Hold on," Isabella turned to the *Letter of Marque*. "Look here." She pointed to the blank lines where the letters were written. "Notice anything unusual?"

"No, not really..." JJ examined the letter.

"I do," Zeke shouted. "Some of the blank lines, where the letters are written..."

"They're longer than the others..." JJ finished Zeke's sentence.

Zeke wrote down the letters above all the long, blank lines. "R-C-E-O-O-Y. Is that a word," he asked.

"Maybe it's a Tocobagan word?" Isabella asked.

"Maybe the word is spelled backward," JJ wondered. "Y-O-O-E-C-R."

"Nah," Zeke shook his head. "That doesn't work either."

"What if we scramble the letters," JJ encouraged. "Y-O-C-R..."

"Yo Creo," Isabella shouted. "It spells Yo Creo!"

"It does?" Zeke asked.

"Hey, you're right, Izzy." JJ pulled the coin from his pocket. "Yo Creo. Just like the doubloon."

"Kermit," Isabella paused. "He said Yo Creo. It means I Believe."

"Yeah, I remember. And Captain Lopez told me that it's important to believe in ourselves if we are to chart the course that is rightly ours to make..." JJ turned to Zeke. "And do you remember what was said in that cable to Major Klearly?"

"About the stolen loot?" Zeke asked.

"No," JJ shook his head. "About the final mystery clue..."

"Not really." Zeke opened his notebook to the written notes on Major Klearly and Lieutenant Dorfman. "But I bet I can find it here...Yeah, here it is. I wrote his exact words:

...Please remind them there is still one more mystery clue to solve. And only then will their journey end where it began. Only then will they be allowed to go home...

"Right. We solved the last clue." JJ agreed, raising the doubloon in the air. "And the journey began with this coin..."

"So if we destroy it," Isabella interrupted his thought. "Maybe toss it in the water...."

"No, you got it all wrong." JJ stopped Isabella short. "I found the doubloon in the artesian well at Fort DeSoto. That's where this whole thing started, right? And that archeologist just told us they just uncovered the old Fort Dade artesian well. Don't you see? That's how the journey ends. Just like Juan Jon Lopez said. *Your journey will end where it began...*"

"I don't know, JJ." Zeke shook his head. "Are you sure..."

"Through the old artesian well," JJ said. "That's our way back. You gotta believe me."

"I believe you, JJ." Isabella reached her arm around JJ and gave him a kiss on the cheek. "You've been right all along this journey. Yo Creo."

"Yeah," Zeke smiled. "Yo Creo."

Chapter Forty

Tale Of The Mystery Doubloon
(2004)

Light swirled in frenzied circles, followed by deafening silence. "Wake up, JJ," Isabella pleaded. "Please wake up!"

"Yo Creo," JJ groaned. "Yo Creo."

He lay prone on the soft sand near Fort DeSoto's beach. The bruise on his forehead, large and purple, throbbed in rhythm to his heartbeat. The sound of power boats, and the splashing surf, magnified the ache in his head.

"I believe..." JJ moaned, still clutching the gold doubloon.

"JJ, please wake up," Isabella whispered again. On bended knees, she held an ice pack in one hand, gently clasping JJ's hand in the other. She pleaded as she pressed the ice on the bruise. "Open your eyes."

"Oh, gawd." Zeke knelt next to Isabella and the other classmates. A look of worry flooded his face as he stared at JJ's limp body. "You'll be okay. All you have to do is wake up and open your eyes."

Mr. Celi stood above Isabella with a worried look on his face. "It's probably just a minor concussion, just like the doctor said..."

"I know he'll be fine," Isabella convinced herself. "I'm sure it's just a bad bruise."

"Where am I?" JJ blinked. The bright sun, hanging high in the sky, silhouetted the classmates towering above him.

"Oh, JJ," Isabella sobbed. "Welcome back..."

"My head..." He slowly sat up to the guarded cheers of his classmates.

"You had me so worried..." Isabella sniffled.

"My head...," he lifted his hand. "...Ouch."

"The doctor says it's not serious," Zeke smiled. "Welcome back. We lost you there for a while. You missed the entire field trip..."

"Ouch," JJ screamed, touching his swollen forehead. "What a headache..."

"Hey JJ. It's me, Mr. Celi. Good thing that doctor came along." He shook his head, smiling. "Don't know how much you remember...I'll let Isabella and Ezekiel tell you what happened...."

"See ya," JJ's classmates shouted.

"Come on kids." Mr. Celi headed back to *Pavillion 29*. "Let's pack up, and get ready for our return on the *Foul Belle*."

****

"*Hey* JJ," Isabella leaned into him. Her blonde curls gently touched his cheek. "You had me really worried..."

"Izzy," JJ smiled. "Nice to be with you. What happened?"

"After you fell in the artesian well," she sniffled, wiping away a tear with her hand. "and after Zeke recovered from his fainting spell..."

"You fainted again?" JJ gave Zeke an astonished look.

"Anyway," Isabella continued. "Zeke ran to get Mr. Celi..."

"He did?" JJ turned to Zeke. "Where'd you find Mr. Celi?"

"At the pavillion with some of the other kids." Zeke shook his head. "But because of your fall, he canceled the trip to Egmont Key."

"Really?" JJ winced. "So we never left *Fort DeSoto*? How is that possible? What about the journey across the Egmont Passage?"

"JJ, please look at me." Isabella gently pulled his chin toward her. "While Zeke went looking for help, a man came along. He carried you up the iron hand-steps of the old well...."

"Who was he?" JJ asked.

"Please listen." She dabbed the water on the dripping ice pack. "Remember the man at *Pavillion 29*...?"

"...He was the same man I interviewed for the *Tidal Tales Telegraph*," Zeke added.

"You were lucky." She smiled, still not believing the coincidence. "He was here to plan this year's annual Gasparilla Days festivities. I didn't know he was a doctor because he was still dressed in his pirate costume..."

"A *doctor*, dressed as a pirate?" JJ sat up, his mind spinning from the head-rush.

"He didn't have a medical bag or anything like that. But he certainly seemed quite calm about the whole situation. He said it was careless of you to have gotten so close to that well." Isabella gave JJ a confused look. "He said you'd be just fine once your head clears up..."

"Izzy," JJ interrupted again. "Who was he?"

"I never asked for his name," Isabella answered. "Everything happened so fast..."

"Do you know?" JJ turned toward Zeke.

"No. Don't think so." Zeke leafed through his notepad. "Nope. During the interview he just referred to himself as the famous French pirate from..."

"You sure you're okay?" Isabella squeezed JJ's shoulder. "What's this all about?"

"I don't remember much right now. But it all seems so strange..." He paused, forcing a weak smile. "But look at this coin? It's the one I found in the well..."

"...Everyone got one," Zeke frowned, dismissing the doubloon in JJ's hand. "Mr. Celi scattered them around Fort DeSoto for us to find. He had a bag full of coins. The doubloons aren't real JJ..."

"Wait a minute." Isabella took the coin, examining it. "This one's not plastic! And something different is written on it. It says, *Yo Creo*. Whatever that means?"

"It means, *I believe*. Someday I'll piece everything together," JJ laughed through the fog in his head. Then, turning to Zeke, he added, "I'll tell you the whole story....give you an exclusive. You can write it up for the *Tidal Tales Telegraph*. Who knows? There might even be enough material for a book..."

"Oh, that reminds me." Isabella reached into her backpack. "Back at the pavillion, Mr. Celi told that French pirate...I mean doctor...that you were a serious pirate buff. That's why he came looking for us, so he could give you this book. He said it's an autographed copy of..."

"Wow!" JJ tore open the white wrapping paper. "Izzy, you read what it says. My vision is still blurry..."

"*Tale Of The Mystery Doubloon*," Isabella read, opening the book to the first page. She then read the inscription:

Always believe in yourself....always! Yo Creo!

A Friend.

Isabella looked up from the book. "Why would he write that?"

"I'm not sure," JJ smiled. "But I think it's part of my adventure across the Egmont Passage..."

"Well I believe you, JJ." Isabella leaned forward, giving him a gentle kiss. "I really do!"

"Thanks, Izzy." JJ's eyes watered. "Yo Creo!"

Epilogue

The trio returned to the *Foul Belle* in preparation for their return to the Bayway Island Boarding School. The smell of stale shrimp, still wafting through the deck of the converted shrimp boat, was a familiar, yet welcome odor. The boat's engine roared to life, pushing the *Foul Belle* away from the wooden docks toward the island school.

Zeke, writing on a deadline, began to piece together his feature story for the *Tidal Tales Telegraph*. Given all the excitement, he wasn't sure what to write, nor where to start.

Sitting next to Sally Jane, Isabella grew tired of hearing how Sally Jane's team won seats next to the mayor for the upcoming Gasparilla Pirate Parade. Isabella, politely excusing herself from the redundant conversation, walked across the deck toward JJ.

"Catching up on your reading?" Isabella gave him a tender smile as she sat next to him on the wooden bench.

"Yeah." JJ returned Isabella's smile. "But my vision is still a bit blurry."

"I believe it." Isabella winced. "That's some bump on the head."

"My new book is quite interesting." JJ lay his head on Isabella's lap. "There are all sorts of cool pirate stories. Just finished a story about an old Spanish galleon sailing in the Gulf of Mexico..."

"Really?" Isabella stroked the hair on JJ's head. "Maybe you'll let me borrow the book when you're finished with it?"

"Sure, Izzy." JJ gave her a contented smile. "Read it now if you'd like. I think I'll take a little rest."

Isabella opened the book, reading the first chapter of JJ's new book. *"The sailor in the crow's nest kept a watchful eye for English ships..."*

JJ, exhausted from his adventure, fell fast asleep. He dreamed that Captain Juan Jon Lopez ordered Jean-Denis and his crewe to draw up the anchor and raise the tattered sails of the *GhostRider*. With the *Jolie Rouge* lowered, the old Spanish galleon caught a February breeze on the Gulf of Mexico. The old ship headed westward toward the horizon, sailing into the mystic....

Florida Timeline

12,400 BC Mastodons, saber- toothed tigers, and giant bison roam the Florida peninsula. By 8,000 the prehistoric animals become extinct.

10,000 BC The world's sea level is about 100 feet lower than today. Following the melt during the Ice Age, Florida is reduced by 200 miles.

3,570 BC The first known Native Americans settle in the Florida area.

1,000 AD The Tocobaga Indians settle in the Pinellas peninsula. By 1710, the culture is destroyed by Spanish exploration and diseases brought from the Europeans.

1492 Christopher Columbus becomes the first European to arrive in the Americas.

1513 Juan Ponce DeLeon arrives in the St. Augustine area. He names the land "Pascua Florida," in honor of the "Feast of Flowers."

1528 Panfilo De Narvaez explores La Florida with an expedition of 600 people. Historians believe he brought the second group of slaves to North America. Narvaez names Tampa Bay, *Bay of the Cross.*

1539	Hernando DeSoto explores Tampa Bay. He renames the bay, *Bay of the Holy Spirit.*
1757	Don Francisco Maria Celi surveys Egmont Key and draws one of the first maps of the area. (Note: Mr. Celi is only fictionally related to Don Celi.)
1776	The 13 original colonies declare their independence from Great Britain, creating the United States of America. *La Florida* is still owned by Spain.
1821	Spain cedes *La Florida* to the United States. Andrew Jackson is named Florida's first governor.
1845	Florida becomes the 27th state of the Union.
1848	The Egmont Key lighthouse is completed in May, only to be destroyed in October by the Great Gale of '48. It will take another ten years to rebuild the lighthouse.
1849	Robert E. Lee, later to be named the commander of the Confederate Army, arrives on Egmont Key to survey it for possible military use.
1860	The Civil War breaks out in the United States. Harriet Tubman, the *Black Moses,* runs the *underground railroad,* funneling runaway slaves from the southern slave states. Many runaways are smuggled to Cuba through the Florida peninsula.
1898	Mullet Key and Egmont Key are militarized in anticipation of the Spanish American War. But Forts DeSoto and Dade never receive enemy fire from the Spanish. Instead, Fort Dade converts to a military hospital for the returning soldiers from Cuba.
1942	Mullet Key is used by the military as an air-to-ground bombing range. Unexploded ordinance will be found at Fort DeSoto through the 1980's.
1963	Fort DeSoto becomes a 900-acre county park, and eventually becomes one of the nation's top-ten beach parks.

1974   *Egmont Key becomes a National Wildlife refuge; in 1989 it becomes a state park.*

1980   *The Summit Venture, a Liberian-registered freighter, crashes into the southbound span of the Sunshine Skyway bridge. The bridge collapses, killing 35 people. A new bridge is completed in 1987.*

1996   *Riots break out in St. Petersburg following the killing of an African American teenager by a white police officer during a traffic stop. To downplay the situation, city officials refer to the riots as "the disturbances."*

2003   *The Tampa Bay Buccaneers make it to the Super Bowl for the first time, defeating the Oakland Raiders by a score of 48-21. The Buccaneers, after a mediocre year, fail to make the playoffs in the 2003-2004 season.*

2004   *JJ, Izzy, and Zeke, complete their journey on the Egmont Passage. On the adventure they meet Billy Barefoot, Victoria, Azaelia, Major Klearly, Lieutenant Dorfman, Corporal Baggs, The Nasty Juan, Jean-Denis Godet, and Kermit The Hermit. Although they are all fictional characters, their memories live on in the minds of the author and his readers.*

Note To My Readers:

There are additional *mysteries* hidden in the pages of this book. Isabella was very wise, but her advice was not her own. Much of the wisdom Isabella shared with JJ and Zeke during their journey through the *Egmont Passage* was inspired by a famous American hero and statesman. The mystery voice in Isabella's advice came from her role model, General Colin L. Powell.

As Secretary of State, Colin Powell is the chief foreign policy advisor to President George W. Bush. When he was Chairman of the Joint Chiefs of Staff, General Powell was the highest ranking military officer in the Unites States Armed Forces. He was also chairman of the board for *America's Promise*, an organization that helps mentor young people. Following is advice that has helped him become successful. See if you can find Isabella's *advice* in Colin Powell's words below. *Yo Creo!*

*Get mad, then get over it (page 39).

*It ain't as bad as you think. It will look better in the morning (page 41).

*Be careful what you choose. You may get it (page 2 & 97).

*Remain calm. Be kind (page 67).

*Don't take counsel of your fears or naysayers (page 83).

*You can't make someone else's choices. You shouldn't let someone make yours (Captain Juan Jon Lopez, page 95).

*Check small things (Kermit The Hermit, page 119).

*Have a vision. Be demanding.

*You have to do the best you can with what you have. So don't let any negative elements in your background be an excuse.

*Share credit.

*It can be done (Yo Creo!)

About The Author

Antonino Fabiano is a middle school Social Studies and
Life Skills teacher for Manatee County Public Schools, in Bradenton,
Florida. He is a retired Air Force officer, freelance writer, and longtime
Parrothead. He holds a Bachelor of Arts degree from the University of
Central Florida, and a Master of Science degree from Troy State University.

While in the military he taught leadership, management, and Air Force
studies at the University of South Florida in Tampa. He served as a public
relations officer at MacDill Air Force Base, also in Tampa. While at the
Pentagon he was a public affairs writer for General Colin L. Powell. In
Valdosta, Georgia he served as managing editor of the weekly base
newspaper.

He is the author of a number of feature stories and poetry. Nino lives
in Tierra Verde, Florida. This is his first novel. Readers may contact him
at TidalTales@aol.com.

ISBN 141201324-0